VICTORIA
MAXWELL

MANiFEST
YOUR
DREAMS

RITUALS and **PRACTICES** for
LIVING YOUR BEST LIFE

HarperCollins*Publishers*

ALSO BY VICTORIA MAXWELL

Witch, Please

HarperCollins*Publishers*
1 London Bridge Street
London SE1 9GF

www.harpercollins.co.uk

HarperCollins*Publishers*
Macken House, 39/40 Mayor Street Upper
Dublin 1, D01 C9W8, Ireland

First published by HarperCollins*Publishers* 2023

1 3 5 7 9 10 8 6 4 2

© Victoria Maxwell 2023

Victoria Maxwell asserts the moral right to
be identified as the author of this work

A catalogue record of this book is
available from the British Library

ISBN 978-0-00-860059-4

Printed and bound by PNB, Latvia

CONTENTS

Introduction   1

PART ONE – WHAT IS MANIFESTATION?
                                                                7

An Introduction to Manifestation   9
The Tough Stuff   19

PART TWO – PREPARING TO MANIFEST
                                                               33

Setting Yourself Up for Success   35
Connecting with Your Heart's True Desires   47
Clearing Blocks to Manifestation   67
You Have the Power!   91

PART THREE – MAKING IT HAPPEN

PART THREE – MAKING IT HAPPEN   117

About the Author   199
Index   200

INTRODUCTION

I've manifested some pretty amazing things over time – large amounts of cash, trips abroad, tickets to sold-out concerts, incredible charity shop finds and expensive jewellery. I've won amazing prizes in Instagram competitions that had thousands of entries, eaten enough free lunches to feed me for a year and I've manifested more books, tarot and oracle decks than I could poke a wand at.

But there's so much more to manifesting than just finding the perfect pair of shoes on sale and in your size (something else I've manifested successfully quite a few times!). When you really start to awaken your manifesting powers, you find that not only can you manifest all the material 'stuff' you want and need, but you can use the same practices to create a life you absolutely love and that is filled with purpose and joy, incredible moments with the people you love and a deeper connection with the truth of who you are and why you're here. And that's better than a free lunch any day!

When you live the life of your dreams you can still manifest all those material goodies if you want them, but they just become the cherry on top of what's already a magical, meaningful and beautiful life.

My journey with manifestation started when I was a child, with letters to Santa (the first manifestation practice for many of us in the western world!) and a bit of prayer. I didn't come from a religious family, but I picked up the prayer basics from somewhere and I went with it. What I asked for or if I even got it, I can't remember now, but it always felt natural and comforting for me to have a chat with some higher power and put my desires out there.

As a teen I discovered Wicca and witchcraft and worked with spells and magic to manifest my desires. That worked incredibly well for me at the time; I was suddenly getting everything I wanted, but not always in the *way* I wanted, and I didn't feel like I could really trust my own magic (yet!). So I took a short break from witchcraft, joined the Church and went back to manifesting through prayer for a little while. In my early twenties, after I left the Church, I got my hands on a copy of *The Secret* by Rhonda Byrne and began to delve into the teachings of the Law of Attraction.

Since then, I've explored and studied various spiritual teachings and paths, including New Age spirituality, various magical paths, the Ascension teachings, ancient Egyptian magic and Reiki and Seichem energy healing. I have also become both a student and teacher of Kundalini yoga, through which I've learned how to manifest using physical movement, meditation, breath, sound vibration and working with the energy bodies.

While I made many wonderful things happen in my life through various forms of manifesting over the years, I also had a lot of questions and concerns about some of the teachings and methods I was coming across. I struggled to get behind the idea that all you had to do was think happy thoughts and a million quid would fall out of the sky, and no one seemed to be talking about the role that privilege, trauma or mental health plays in manifestation.

As someone with anxiety who often struggles to keep my thoughts high-vibe 100 per cent of the time, but still successfully manifests amazing things in my life, I knew there had to be more to it. Over the years I've come up with my own set of ideas about all this and found ways to navigate it, all of which I'm going to share with you in this book. But what I do know for sure is that no one has all the answers. The best way to work with manifestation is however works for you. It's my intention that this book will help you find your own magical way to manifest your dreams.

As well as all the 'stuff', I've also manifested some of my biggest dreams. I created a successful spiritual business, which meant I could quit my day job and do what I love for a living. I manifested a book deal, and seeing my first book *Witch, Please: Empowerment and Enlightenment for the Modern Mystic* on the bookshelf was something I had visualised for many years before it happened! Since then, I've manifested another *five* publishing deals, which still just blows me away! I've also manifested so many wonderful people into my life and I can still remember the exact practice I used to manifest my husband (crying on the floor after a bad date and writing down all the traits I wanted in a partner – try it for yourself!). I even got my dream Las Vegas wedding! I currently live in a beautiful home with a big office filled with books and space to do yoga. My fridge and my heart are both full, and I feel abundant and prosperous, and I hold so much gratitude for everything I have.

But it wasn't always like this. There was a time when I had so little money in my bank account that the cashier tore up my withdrawal slip right in front of me (back in the days when those were a thing!). I've been on benefits, slept on friends' floors – and I even lived in a tent for a little while. I had jobs that felt like they were sucking the life out of me, and romantic relationships that were absolutely disastrous. I struggled to pay rent, got into debt, and at times felt deeply miserable, lost and alone.

And while I know that even then I still had a lot of privilege and much to be grateful for – a roof (or tarp!) over my head, friends who let me crash at theirs' and I never went hungry – things certainly feel a lot better and easier now.

I've never felt more at peace with who I am and where I am in life. I feel so incredibly blessed for the life I'm living, the life I have manifested, and while I still have bad days, hard days and the occasional visit from my old pal anxiety, I really do feel like I'm living the life that I used to dream of.

Wherever you are in life right now, I want you to know that things *can* get better. You really *can* manifest your dreams, and this book can be your guide on the journey.

HOW TO WORK WITH THIS BOOK

Your manifesting journey is yours to walk in the way that is right for you. Use this book as an inspirational life coach or a magical companion by your side.

Each section will look at different aspects of the manifestation process, including working out what you really want, clearing blocks to manifestation and activating your manifesting power, as well as plenty of my favourite manifesting practices and rituals. I invite you to read the sections in this book in order, so you're in the best place possible for your manifestation work. However, only take what resonates for you. Part of living the life of your dreams means using your intuition and going where you're guided. If a certain section, practice or ritual doesn't interest or apply to you, skip to the next one. You can always come back to it later if you feel called.

As you read through this book you'll notice lots of opportunities to *Grab your Journal!* When you reach these sections, take out your journal and answer the questions. You can write as much or as little as you like. You can even pull an oracle or tarot card on each question if you have a deck on hand.

Journalling can help you uncover so much more about your own thoughts and feelings, and it can shine light on aspects of your inner world that you may not even be aware of. Journalling is a valuable part of the process and really recommended; however, if you find it doesn't work for you, instead take some time to think about or meditate on the questions. You could even find a friend who wants to go on this journey with you, then you can chat about your answers together.

It's your time to shine.
It's time to live your most magical life.
It's time to manifest your dreams.

I wish you so much love, luck and success on this journey. May all your dreams come true and may everything you manifest light up your heart, your life and the world around you.

With so much love,

Vix

x

PART ONE

WHAT IS MANIFESTATION?

AN INTRODUCTION TO MANIFESTATION

Manifestation simply means *to make something happen*. You're manifesting whenever you move a thought, idea or dream into physical reality.

Manifestation is nothing new; every spiritual path or religion have their own take on how to make things happen. In many major religions, prayer (asking the gods for what you want) is essentially a manifestation practice. In Wicca, witchcraft and other nature-based or magical paths, practitioners work with spells to manifest their desires. As with prayer, spellwork can also involve calling on a higher power (usually a god, goddess or other deity), but magical practitioners also manifest through connecting to their own power and the power of nature. In many Buddhist and Yogic traditions there is a focus on manifesting for the good of all rather than on what the ego-self desires. Those who are on a yogic path work with meditation, breath, mantra and asana (physical poses and practices) to achieve higher consciousness and, with it, the ability to create or attract what is needed in life. In the New Thought and Theosophy teachings that gained popularity in the late 1800s, people began to work with traditional spiritual practices alongside the power of the mind and positive thinking to create the outcomes they desired.

Most manifestation practices we come across in modern spirituality have their roots in these ancient teachings.

HOW DOES MANIFESTATION WORK?

There are four main elements to manifestation:

- *Thoughts*
- *Action*
- *Vibration*
- *Divine assistance*

When these four things are working in alignment it's almost impossible *not* to live the life of your dreams.

There may be times when you're able to manifest something using just one or two of these elements, but working with all four puts you into a deeper alignment with your desires and enhances your chances of successful manifesting.

Having these four keys, or ways, into manifestation also means that if you're struggling in one area – for example, if you are finding it hard to keep your thoughts aligned to what you want (something that's tough for many of us at times) – you could do what you can with your thoughts but also work on calling on divine assistance or taking physical action and still experience great success with your manifesting.

THOUGHTS

Manifestation usually begins with your thoughts, ideas, dreams and visions. The mind is also the place where we hold a lot of blocks.

Aligning your thoughts for manifestation includes:

- *Identifying and releasing limiting beliefs and blocks.*
- *Setting intentions.*
- *Making decisions.*
- *Aligning your thoughts with what you want.*
- *Positive thinking.*
- *Developing self-belief.*
- *Logically and rationally working out what you want and how to make it happen.*

ACTION

Once you've figured out what you want, you can then take action to make it happen.

Taking action includes:

- *Asking for what you want.*
- *Asking for help.*
- *Moving your intention into physical form.*
- *Acting on your decisions.*
- *Working towards your goals.*
- *Walking your talk.*
- *Showing up.*

- *Following intuitive nudges.*
- *Meeting the universe halfway.*
- *Doing the groundwork.*

VIBRATION

Your vibration is the vibe or energy that you project out into the world. Your thoughts (conscious and subconscious), words and actions create your vibration, along with your intentions, your heart, your emotions, your chakras, aura and all the spiritual, energetic and personal development work you do on yourself.

Aligning your vibration for manifestation includes:

- *Activating and expanding your aura.*
- *Aligning your chakras.*
- *Speaking about yourself and others positively.*
- *Connecting to your heart's true desires.*
- *Opening your heart.*
- *Connecting to your emotions.*
- *Listening to your intuition.*
- *Clearing, protecting and grounding yourself.*
- *Aligning with your highest self and soul self.*
- *Working on your confidence and self-esteem.*
- *Choosing kindness and compassion.*

DIVINE ASSISTANCE

Your relationship to divine assistance will be personal to you, but this is where we look to a force greater than ourselves for guidance and support in our manifesting. Working with divine assistance can help you to align your desires and outcomes to your soul's true calling, purpose and the highest divine will.

If you don't resonate with this idea, divine assistance can simply be about awakening your own inner divine power.

Working with divine assistance can include:

- *Calling on a god, goddess, the divine, source, universe, universal love or whatever term resonates with you.*
- *Calling on angels, archangels, ascended masters, gods, goddesses and other deities.*
- *Working with your personal spirit guides.*
- *Prayer.*
- *Having faith.*
- *Working with altars and devotional practices.*
- *Connecting with your own higher self, soul self, mighty I AM presence and inner divine spark of light.*
- *Connecting with the divine light within and owning your power.*

When you have these elements working together, you're essentially bringing your mind, heart, body and spirit into balance. You can then connect with your heart's true desire, align your thoughts, words and vibration to it, take action towards it and know you have divine assistance at your side that is helping to make it happen.

GRAB YOUR JOURNAL!

- *What is your personal definition of manifestation?*
- *What is one wonderful thing you've already manifested? How did you do it?*
- *What is something you've struggled to manifest? Why do you think that is?*
- *Who do you call on or create with in your manifesting? Is it a higher power outside of you, the power within you, or both?*
- *Are there any divine helpers you'd like to start working with? (See page 110 for ideas!)*

MANIFESTATION MYTHS

There are a few myths that surround the practice of manifestation, and here are some of the most common ones to be aware of:

MYTH 1: YOU CAN MANIFEST ABSOLUTELY ANYTHING YOU WANT!

While it's true that you can manifest *almost* anything, you also have to take into account things like the law of physics, the limitations of the physical body, your own readiness and ability to make it happen and whether or not it's really in alignment with your best and highest good (more on that later!).

MYTH 2: IF YOU CAN'T MANIFEST IT, IT'S YOUR FAULT.

There are a million different reasons why your manifestation might not be working, and blaming yourself (or blaming others for where they're at on their manifesting journey) is rarely helpful in any way. If your manifesting isn't working, take a break, take a breath, let go of self-blame and keep reading this book.

MYTH 3: THERE'S ONE SPECIFIC METHOD OF MANIFESTATION THAT WORKS FOR EVERYONE.

If this were true, everyone would be using it and getting everything they wanted. There are numerous different methods and practices, many of which you'll find in this book, but it's all about finding what works for you.

MYTH 4: IF YOU HAVE MENTAL HEALTH ISSUES YOU WON'T BE ABLE TO MANIFEST, SINCE IT'S ALL ABOUT POSITIVE THINKING.

While positive thinking can definitely help you manifest your dream life, it's just one way to keep your vibration high. Another approach is through self-love and being kind to yourself through your challenges.

MYTH 5: YOU ATTRACT EVERYTHING THAT HAPPENS TO YOU, GOOD AND BAD.

We live in a world of duality and everyone experiences good times and challenging times. We all suffer, we all feel pain (emotional or physical) and we all have bad days. Sometimes we do play a part in the creation of our own suffering, and we then have an opportunity to learn from it and make changes. Other times our difficulties are caused by other people or situations that are completely out of our control. There can be a fine line between taking responsibility for your own actions and blaming yourself for something that happened to you, but there's nothing high-vibe about victim-blaming yourself. Look for lessons and opportunities for growth but never blame yourself for the actions of others, for what is out of your control or mistakes you made in the past that are now behind you.

MYTH 6: BEING GOOD AT MANIFESTING MEANS YOU'RE MORE SPIRITUAL OR ENLIGHTENED.

Spirituality and enlightenment is not a competition.

MYTH 7: MANIFESTING IS MATERIALISTIC.

Manifesting practices and rituals can absolutely be used to bring more material things into your life, but the real magic happens when you manifest a life you love.

MYTH 8: IF YOU THINK A NEGATIVE THOUGHT IT WILL MANIFEST.

The reason why working on your own thoughts is important is because it sets off a chain reaction. If you don't check yourself, your thoughts become your words, your words become your actions and your actions create your life experience. But most of us would never take action on our intrusive, anxious, dark or bizarre random thoughts. Your thoughts are powerful, but so is what's in your heart. The universe knows your heart and no negative thought can override the truth of your heart.

Try to work with your thoughts as much as you can, get professional help if your thoughts are becoming a problem for you, but remember manifesting is about intention. If your true intentions are aligned with love, don't worry so much about every negative thought you have.

Manifesting with assistance from your divine helpers can also keep you safe from manifesting anything through your thoughts that you don't really want on a soul and heart level.

MYTH 9: YOU CAN MANIFEST BY JUST THINKING ABOUT WHAT YOU WANT.

When you get your thoughts clear and aligned on what you want and set the intention to make it happen, those thoughts begin to become part of your vibration. When you have a strong desire to do something you'll start taking action towards it whether you're consciously aware of it or not. When your thoughts are aligned with your heart and your best and highest good, divine assistance often steps in to help. So, it may seem as though you're just thinking about what you want and getting it, but all elements are usually in play.

GRAB YOUR JOURNAL!

What are some of the myths or things you've heard about manifesting that haven't resonated with you?

THE TOUGH STUFF

In this section we're going to explore some of the tough questions around manifestation that don't always get addressed. Pour yourself a cup of hot cocoa and get cosy as we spill some magical tea over some important issues.

PRIVILEGE

Talking about privilege can be tough because it brings up such intense emotion for most of us. But this is exactly why it's an important part of the manifestation process.

How you feel about your own privilege, or lack thereof, can have a huge impact on your ability to manifest something better for yourself.

Identifying and acknowledging where you sit on the spectrum of privilege doesn't need to be a guilt or blame game. We are all born into a certain level of privilege. For some, that's a head-start in society, while others are beginning on a back foot.

We all have our own personal ideas about why this happens. Some spiritual people believe that we choose our parents and are born into the perfect situation for our soul growth and purpose in this lifetime. This is, of course, easier to believe when you're born into a loving home and have all your needs met.

Maybe it's all part of a divine higher plan or maybe it's just a random roll of the cosmic dice, but whatever your thoughts and beliefs around all this are, we can't escape the fact that we live in a world where some people face challenges that others do not.

Doing some work on ourselves, our mindset around privilege and hopefully even looking at how we can help those less privileged than us are all things that elevate our personal consciousness and actually make manifesting our own best and highest life much easier.

If you have a certain amount of privilege, you may feel guilt and shame around having more than others. If you don't believe you deserve what you already have, how can you possibly manifest more for yourself?

If you have less privilege than others, you may feel some blame and anger towards those who have more than you do. Beliefs around rich people not deserving what they have can be a huge block if you're trying to manifest more wealth for yourself. If you subconsciously can't stand rich people, it can be hard to visualise yourself living a more abundant and prosperous life and being happy.

Most people will resonate with both of these examples to some extent. No matter how much you have, there's always someone who has more, and no matter how much you're struggling, there's always someone worse off.

So, while the privilege conversation is tough to have, it can hold the key for many of our conscious or subconscious beliefs that block us from manifesting a life full of blessings for ourselves, our families, our communities and in the wider world.

GRAB YOUR JOURNAL!

- *Can you think of any privileges you have? How do you feel about them?*
- *What emotions come up for you around this topic?*
- *What beliefs or judgements do you have about those who have more than you do?*
- *What beliefs or judgements do you have about those who have less than you do?*
- *Now re-write those beliefs as positive statements, e.g. 'I don't believe rich people deserve what they have' could be re-written as, 'We all deserve to be prosperous and abundant, and that includes me!'*

CAPITALISM AND CONSUMERISM

When everything has a price, money certainly makes life easier, and there is nothing wrong with wanting to manifest enough money to create more comfortable lives for ourselves and our loved ones. But our cultural obsession with the rich and famous can often have us wondering how much exactly is 'enough'.

We watch how the other half (or rather, the one per cent) live via reality TV shows, we follow them on social media and maybe pick up the odd tabloid magazine for an insight into their worlds. We watch as they publicly battle with online hate, addiction, exhaustion, relationship breakdowns and mental health issues. If a few million pounds could solve all our problems, why is it that so many people with large amounts of wealth, success, power and material goods are just as unhappy and unfulfilled as everyone else? That's not to say you can't be happy and rich, but perhaps extreme wealth doesn't create happiness.

Many of us have some concerns about capitalism – the disparity of wealth, too much power in the hands of a few, exploitation of workers and the environment and excess consumerism. But we're beginning to realise that filling our closets and our homes with stuff we don't need doesn't make us feel more fulfilled; in fact, it can make us feel more overwhelmed, not to mention what it does to our bank accounts. We're also starting to understand the true environmental and exploitative cost of our obsession with fast fashion, the beauty industry, new gadgets and all the other 'things' we pick up while we're out shopping that end up unused, unloved and in a bag for the charity shop a few months later.

But capitalism can also provide us with opportunities to pursue our dreams, to re-train or study, to get ahead in our careers, start our own businesses, own our own homes, and offer us plenty of choices as to how, where and with whom we spend our money.

We all have our own thoughts and opinions about these big issues. The invitation here is for you to simply consider the role that capitalism and consumerism may play in the manifesting of your desires.

Maybe you really do want your own TV show or to become a billionaire, or maybe you just want to quit society, go off grid, take up van life or move to an ashram. Whatever you want to manifest is totally up to you, but making sure you are manifesting what you really want and need – and not what society is telling you to want or not want – is part of the secret to manifesting a life you really love and feel excited about.

TRAUMA

The more we learn about trauma, the more we understand that everyone has it to some extent. Whether it's trauma with a big T or a little t, it can impact our ability to manifest our dreams. Trauma affects the nervous system, it puts us in flight-or-fight mode, it affects our self-esteem and feelings of safety, security and self-worth, and these things can all impact your ability to create a wonderful life for yourself.

Having trauma doesn't mean you can't still manifest your dreams, it just means that you may need some extra support to do so. If you find you're keeping yourself safe by not taking action towards your dreams, if you are struggling to believe that you can actually make your dreams happen, or you just know you have some big stuff to work out, do something to support your healing alongside your manifesting journey. Try counselling, talking therapy, read some books on trauma or find a group with whom you can share your experiences.

TOXIC POSITIVITY

A little positivity can go a long way when it comes to manifestation. When you think and speak positively about yourself and others it shifts your vibration, and you start to view the world from a more positive perspective. People are more drawn to those who have a positive outlook on life, and when it comes to manifesting love, friends and work opportunities, projecting positivity rather than complaining and always seeing the worst can make a huge difference.

There is, however, a big difference between working on a positive mindset and veering off into toxic positivity.

When you're on the journey to manifesting your dreams, you are still allowed to have bad days. It's okay to be upset when things don't go to plan. You can be angry and frustrated at the world. You can grieve when you lose something or someone. You will likely feel the full spectrum of human emotion.

Toxic positivity is an attempt to ignore or bypass our own uncomfortable feelings, and the challenges of others, in the pursuit of constantly staying high-vibe. But the most high-vibrational thing you can do is give yourself permission to be human. To sit with and love yourself through the difficult times and tough emotions, to get support if you need it and to work with what comes up in whatever way works for you.

LAW OF ATTRACTION

The Law of Attraction is the idea that what you project out into the world is what you get back. It can absolutely be used to manifest your dreams, and we'll dive deeper into it later in this book, but it's important to remember that the Law of Attraction is just one law of the universe.

There are times when you need to take responsibility for what you put out into the universe, but there are also times to release self-blame, to realise that not everything is your fault, and to let it go. Knowing where the line is between these two spaces can be a challenge, and wherever yours is will be deeply personal to you.

Whatever you choose to believe about the Law of Attraction will be your personal truth; however, as we move into a *new* New Age, many of us now believe it's time to let go of the idea that we've somehow manifested the harm that has been caused to us. When someone has been harmed, hurt, abused, bullied, victimised, traumatised or controlled, that is always the fault of the person inflicting that action, never the fault of the victim.

The Law of Free Will is also in effect, and with eight billion people on this planet all making their own choices, sometimes their decisions will affect us. How we choose to deal with it when it happens is where the magic and our power lies.

Work with the Law of Attraction, become what you want to receive, but remember the Law of Attraction is just one way by which energy works.

KARMA AND DHARMA

Karma is a Sanskrit word that has traditionally been used to describe the cosmic baggage we accumulate in this life and in our past lives that we must in some way 'pay off'. Similar to the Law of Attraction, there's an element to karma of attracting what you deserve – what goes around comes around – but karma is so much more than this. Karma is an energetic imprint of where we've been, what we've done and what we're carrying forward.

We all have karma or baggage to clear, to unpack, to work through. We have lifetimes of 'stuff' that we carry through incarnations, but in every moment that we make a new, better choice, in every moment that we choose love, kindness and compassion towards ourselves or others we are clearing and healing our own karma.

Who we were and where we've been is not just baggage, it is also a blessing. There is so much we can learn from the past, so many blessings that can help propel us forward. Karma is not all heavy, it is also light, joy, love and magic!

Dharma, another Sanskrit word, is similar in concept to life purpose, but can also translate as 'rightful duty' or 'righteous living'. Dharma, and even the idea of a life purpose, may seem like it locks you into a certain path, but it's really about finding your true nature, your highest destiny, and expressing that fully in this lifetime.

When it comes to manifestation there is sometimes a belief that your karma can stop you from manifesting something wonderful in your life, but if you are aligned with your dharma, your purpose, you will be able to manifest everything that is in alignment with your true divine nature. You may not always get what your ego or personality self wants, but you will always be able to manifest what your soul desires. And when you do, you'll find true peace and happiness.

GRAB YOUR JOURNAL!

- *What are your thoughts on karma?*
- *Is there anything you're feeling called to do to clear your slate?*
- *Do you believe in the idea of dharma?*
- *What is your true divine nature?*

MANIFESTING AND MENTAL HEALTH

You can still manifest magic in your life if you have issues with your mental health. The key to unlocking your manifesting power may not be in keeping your mindset 100 per cent positive or in always keeping your vibration high (I don't know anyone, even incredibly successful people, who never come down once in a while!). As we mentioned in the previous section, there are other ways to activate your power. Call on the divine, on your guides, angels, ancestors or whoever you feel connected with, and ask them to help you with your manifesting.

Saint Dymphna is the patron saint of mental health, depression and anxiety and she is a wonderful guide to call on for extra support. As well as seeking support in the physical world, ask Saint Dymphna to hold you through whatever is coming up for her. Ask her to guide you to the right people, resources and situations that can support you.

Working with magical tools can also be really helpful. As long as you can state your intention out loud, your tools can then hold your intention on your behalf.

Remember, you can manifest in many different ways, so find what works for you, and let go of any old stories and beliefs that tell you otherwise.

THE EGO

The key to manifesting your best and highest life is to manifest from the heart rather than the ego. The ego is not a bad thing – in fact, you need it to survive. There are many different definitions of ego, but it's basically the part of you that's focused on the self. The ego makes sure you're safe, that your basic survival is covered, but it's not always that useful when it comes to manifesting your dreams.

The ego can go on a trip at times, convincing you that you're more special and deserving than others, but it can also tell you to play small, be quiet, fit in. The ego just wants you to be safe, it doesn't realise that by fitting in you may miss out on living *your* truth.

Being able to notice when you're in ego and when you're in heart is so important when manifesting. Your heart knows your truth. Your heart knows your higher plan and will always guide you towards more love, light, peace, happiness and joy.

Manifesting from the heart really just means identifying and clearing away any thoughts or ideas that might be coming from safety and not from love so you can manifest from the highest, most loving, aligned place deep within you.

THE HEART BREATH

Put your hand on your heart and close your eyes. Take three deep breaths, inhaling and exhaling at the heart. Visualise a glowing gold and pink light in the centre of your heart. Let this light pulse and grow and expand as you keep your intention and awareness at your heart space.

Take a few more deep breaths focusing on the light in your heart. Now ask your heart, what do you want?

GRAB YOUR JOURNAL!

Write down anything that comes through.

This is a very simple exercise that you can do at any time to help you get out of your head and/or ego and into your heart. You may receive simple answers or messages from your heart through words or phrases, visions or ideas, or you may just get a feeling or sense of knowing. The more often you do this, the easier it will be to connect with your heart.

CONSCIOUS MANIFESTATION

Conscious manifesting occurs in two ways:

1. *You start to become aware of just how much you're manifesting in every moment through your thoughts, words, actions and vibrations.*
2. *You become more conscious about what you call into your life through your manifestation practices and rituals.*

We are manifesting all the time, in every moment. Every decision we make, every action we take, no matter how small, is creating our life experience.

TRY THIS

Set an alarm on your phone at five moments during the day. When the alarm goes off, take a moment to check in with yourself. Check your thoughts, your emotions, your vibrations and your actions, then ask yourself, 'What am I manifesting in this moment?'

Keep doing this practice until you feel yourself becoming more aware of how and what you're manifesting through the day.

When it comes to conscious manifesting through practices and rituals, one of the best things you can do before you start is to ask yourself *why* you want to manifest this. Tune into your own heart and check if it's really what you want or if there is something else that could bring you even more joy, love or whatever else you need.

When manifesting material items, pause and consider:

- *Where does this item come from?*
- *Who made it?*
- *What impact does this item have on the lives of others and on the planet?*
- *What impact will it have on me, both now and in the future?*

After asking these questions and doing a little research you may find that the item you wanted is made by a company that doesn't have the same values as you and it's no longer a good match for your vibration.

Conscious manifesting doesn't mean you can't have nice things. Luckily, there are many companies that are creating ethical goods and many making positive changes. Supporting small, local, secondhand, eco-friendly and/or sustainable businesses when you can is not only good for your aura and home but also good for the soul and the planet.

Conscious manifesting simply means manifesting what is in alignment with your heart, soul and values.

HOW TO MANIFEST IN A CHALLENGING WORLD

The world is not without its challenges and the truth is, no one has it figured out. You can tie yourself up in knots about the state of the world, give up on your dreams because not everyone has the ability to manifest theirs, and fall into a pit of despair. And fair enough, because as compassionate human beings we all go there at times. But denying your own power, potential and ability to make a difference in the world helps no one. To give up on your dreams because not everyone else can fulfil theirs doesn't help you, your family, your friends or your community, and it definitely doesn't help the world.

If you have an opportunity to make a better life for yourself and those around you, the best thing you can do is to take it.

Here are some tips I've found useful on my journey:

- *Instead of feeling guilty for what you have, try to get into gratitude.*
- *Manifest what you need so you can make a positive difference in the lives of others.*
- *Manifest abundance and prosperity, then be generous with it.*
- *Make changes in your own life that align with your heart.*
- *Keep doing the work on yourself and educating yourself about the issues the world is facing.*
- *Learn about the issues that affect your local communities, and if you can, do something to help.*
- *Instead of trying to fix the whole world, just work on your small part of it.*
- *Inspire others to manifest the life of their dreams.*
- *Learn to rest, not quit.*

PART TWO

PREPARING TO MANIFEST

SETTING YOURSELF UP FOR SUCCESS

SELF-LOVE

Self-love is an essential practice on the path to manifesting your dreams. When you really believe you are worthy and deserving of living your best life, it's so much easier to manifest it!

Self-love is:

- *Speaking to and about yourself with kindness.*
- *Giving yourself permission to just be yourself.*
- *Being grateful for your body and all it does for you.*
- *Knowing you are beautiful inside and out.*
- *Self-forgiveness.*
- *Putting yourself first so you have the energy and ability to help others.*
- *Believing in yourself.*
- *Knowing you are worthy and deserving of your dreams.*
- *Making yourself a priority.*

MIRROR WORK

A simple practice to do in tandem with your manifestation practices is to look in the mirror every day and tell yourself *I love you*. You can tell yourself how fantastic you are, how amazing you look, anything else that feels good. You can always start with something small if that feels like it's too much. Tell yourself thanks for showing up today, or that your hair looks great, or give yourself a pep talk. Say something kind to yourself in the mirror daily and see how your self-love grows.

SELF-CARE

Looking after yourself is non-negotiable if you really want to manifest a magical life. When you care for yourself, you feel better, and when you feel better it's easier to see the path ahead to even better things.

Self-care is:

- *Getting enough sleep and rest.*
- *Drinking enough water.*
- *Eating nourishing food.*
- *Physical exercise.*
- *Spending time outside.*
- *Meditation and mindfulness.*
- *Going for health checks.*
- *Keeping your home tidy.*
- *Taking breaks from social media.*
- *Setting strong, loving boundaries with others.*

- *Being kind to yourself.*
- *Connecting with safe and supportive people.*
- *Booking in for a massage, reiki treatment or tarot reading.*
- *Making time for your hobbies and interests outside of work.*
- *Whatever else it is for you!*

GRAB YOUR JOURNAL!

Write down three to five self-care practices that are non-negotiable to you. Make sure at least one is something you aren't doing regularly yet but would like to start doing.

Make a note of these on your calendar or somewhere you'll see them often as a reminder.

RAISING YOUR VIBRATION

Raising your vibration really just means getting yourself into an energetic mental, emotional and spiritual state where you feel good. When you feel good you become a magnet for attracting more good things. You become open to opportunities and are more likely to feel inspired and energised to take action towards your dreams and goals.

Raising your vibe isn't about ignoring or bypassing your true emotional state. Remember, sometimes the most high-vibrational thing you can do is to give yourself the grace to be where you are.

But in those moments when you find yourself being critical of yourself or others, when you're in a loop of negative thinking or are just feeling a bit flat, try raising your vibration and see what happens!

Here are some ideas of ways you can start to raise your vibration right now:

- *Make a high-vibrational playlist with songs that light you up. Listen, dance and sing along to it often!*
- *Put your hand on your heart and take a deep breath. It's so simple but it works like magic.*
- *Connect with people who make you feel good when they are around.*
- *Write yourself a love note and put it somewhere you'll find it later.*
- *Tidy your space.*
- *Create a sacred space.*
- *Look in the mirror and pick three things you love about yourself.*
- *Say something nice to a total stranger; tell them you like their shoes or comment on someone's social post, telling them how awesome you think they are.*
- *Send a voice note or a GIF to someone you love.*
- *Watch a movie or TV show that you loved as a kid.*
- *Go outside.*
- *Shake your body. Just get up and shake out all the negativity you've been holding.*
- *Visualise a gold ray of light coming down into your crown chakra at the top of your head and filling your entire being with high-vibrational gold light.*
- *Affirm, say:* I believe in myself. My life is magical. I am living a high-vibrational life, *three times.*
- *Visualise yourself wrapped in golden light while you meditate or take a nap.*

- *Carry a shiny crystal in your pocket.*
- *Wear clothes you feel good in.*
- *Tell someone you love them.*
- *Remember that you are a being of light having a human experience.*
- *Practise gratitude.*
- *Help someone in need or help someone else to raise their vibration.*
- *Whatever else makes you feel good!*

GRAB YOUR JOURNAL!

- *Write about a time when you just felt like you were in a high-vibrational state. What was happening in that moment?*
- *Write about a time when you got something you really wanted. What was your emotional state then?*
- *Write a list of five things you can do any time you want to raise your vibration. Make a copy of this list and put it somewhere you'll be able to refer to it when you need it.*

HIGH-VIBE WATER RITUAL

This is so easy to do, and you can do it anywhere and at any time, as long as you can get your hands on a glass or a bottle of water. You can also use this ritual with your tea or any other beverages.

You will need:

- *Glass or a bottle of water (or any other preferred drink)*
- *Pen (optional)*

1. *Hold the water in both hands at heart level.*
2. *Close your eyes, if you can (this is optional if people are watching!). Visualise pink light from your heart opening up and expanding into the water. Visualise gold light from above you filling the water like sunlight on the ocean. Visualise the water being filled with your loving intentions and high-vibrational frequencies of light.*
3. *With a pen, your finger or just by visualising it, write a high-vibrational word or phrase on the glass or bottle. Try something like good vibes, high vibes, happy and joyful – whatever resonates with you.*
4. *Now take a sip and drink those high vibes!*

HIGH-VIBE VISUALISATION

Visualise a ball of golden light at your feet. As you inhale, see the ball of light drawing a spiral of light in an upwards direction all around you. As you visualise this spiral rising up, see it transmuting any negativity, any low energy, and really feel it lifting your spirits, your mood and your vibration. On the exhale, just bask in this golden light. Repeat this spiral from the bottom as many times as you like.

GRATITUDE

One of the biggest keys to unlocking the life of your dreams is gratitude. When you're focused on manifesting all the things you want for your life, it can be easy to forget to live in the present moment and to enjoy the here and now. If you're not in the habit of practising gratitude, when your manifestations do take physical form it may be easy to miss them, or you may be so focused on the next thing that you don't stop and appreciate what you've already manifested. This can lead to a never-ending loop of always wanting more and never feeling like you have enough no matter how many wonderful things you create in your life.

You can still be working towards your dreams while also enjoying every wonderful second of your life here and now. Gratitude is also one of the quickest ways to raise your vibration, which means the more joy, peace and presence you find in the present moment, the easier it is to manifest more of that!

Manifestation is just one part of living a magical life. Don't wait until all your dreams have come true before you start living and enjoying your life. Start right here, right now. You are on the path, more good things are coming your way, but it will be easier to notice them, feel and appreciate them, when you appreciate where you are right now.

What you're grateful for can be big or small, it doesn't matter. Maybe you're grateful for family and friends, for food in the fridge, cups of tea or sunrises. Maybe you're grateful you found this book! And if you can't think of anything else, you can always just be grateful for today.

A PRAYER OF GRATITUDE

Start the day with this prayer and see how it changes your energy. (Feel free to change the words to suit you!)

> Dear divine spirit, spirit guides and angels, thank you for this day. Thank you for everything I have and everything I am. Thank you for helping me use everything I have and everything I am to make a positive difference in this world, in the hearts and lives of others and within myself. And so it is.

GRAB YOUR JOURNAL!

- *Write down some of your dreams that have already come true.*
- *Think back to a time when you wanted what you have now. How does it feel now that you have this?*
- *How will you celebrate and show gratitude for everything wonderful that you manifest in your life?*

GRATITUDE PRACTICES

Here are some simple gratitude practices to help you live and love your life in the here and now.

GRATITUDE JOURNAL

In a dedicated gratitude journal, write down three to five things that you're grateful for each day. You can do this at night and reflect on the day that was, or in the morning to help you get into a grateful state for the day ahead.

GRATITUDE JAR

Each day take a small piece of paper, write down something you are grateful for and put it into a jar. When the jar is full, or any time you feel like you could use a little reminder of what's wonderful in your life, pull out a gratitude or two and read them. Put them back in the jar so you can read them again later or start a new jar when it's full. This can be a nice practice to do with your family or the people you live with, if they are open to it.

MORNING PRACTICE

When you wake up in the morning, ideally before you get out of bed, or while you're in the shower or on your commute, say out loud or in your head the things you're grateful for. Go for as long as you can, or set yourself a daily target for three, five or ten things a day.

NIGHT PRACTICE

As you're closing your eyes about to go to sleep, list the things you're grateful for from the day. This is much more effective than counting sheep and helps to put you in a relaxed, happy state as you drift off to dreamland.

EXPRESSING GRATITUDE

As you go about your day, express your gratitude often. If you see a nice sunrise, say to yourself, or others around you, *What a beautiful sunrise.* When you're enjoying your morning coffee, say, *This coffee is delicious.* When spending time with loved ones, say, *I'm having such a wonderful time.* You can do this whether there's anyone to listen to you or not. Sit on the couch alone and say out loud, *I love this TV show!* Do this for 24 hours and see what happens. You might feel like a goofball, but you should feel like a pretty happy goofball!

The more you do this the more it just becomes second nature to notice and appreciate all the good things in your life. Expressing your gratitude is powerful; it makes other people feel good, it makes you feel good, and it helps you to really anchor into each beautiful moment of your life.

PHOTO ALBUM

If you're into photography or just like taking photos on your phone, take photos of the things you're grateful for and create a gratitude album. Take photos of beautiful days, books you've loved, time spent with friends, any precious moments no matter how small. Set a goal to take at least one gratitude photo a day to help you to seek out and notice more things to be grateful for.

SCRAP BOOK

Make a scrap book including photos (as above), but also include things like concert tickets, invitations, restaurant receipts, pressed flowers, cards featuring beautiful quotes or artwork, anything that helps you connect with the memories and gratitude from the special days and moments in your life.

GRATITUDE EXPLOSION

Make a list of 100 things you're grateful for. Write quickly, don't overthink it. Let yourself just free-write anything and everything that comes to mind.

This is a great practice for spiritually powerful days like the equinox or solstice, full moons or any time you are feeling a little flat and could use a reminder of all the wonderful things in your life. If 100 feels like too many, aim for 50 or even 20, then work up to 100. Once you get really good at this, try writing 150 or 222! Then put the list somewhere you can return to it any time you need a gratitude boost.

LAW OF GRACE

The Law of Grace is essentially a failsafe for your manifesting. If you are trying to manifest something that could potentially harm you or others, take you off on a path that isn't in your best interest or just isn't in alignment with your soul's true purpose and desire, the Law of Grace will protect you.

All you need to do is add: *I manifest this under the Law of Grace, and so it is* at the end of any ritual or practice you do and you can rest assured that your manifestation will be protected.

There are other versions of the Law of Grace you can also use. For something more witchy, try: *And if it harms none, so mote it be.* Or you can always just ask: *May this manifest in alignment with my best and highest good, and the best and highest good of all, and so it is.*

CONNECTING WITH YOUR HEART'S TRUE DESIRES

Manifesting from the heart is the best way to create a life you absolutely love. In this section we'll look at how to connect deeper with your heart's true desires and how to identify and release what isn't an energetic match for your own heart.

FIGURING OUT WHAT YOU REALLY WANT

One of the most important but sometimes difficult parts of manifesting your dreams is to figure out what your dreams actually are. Perhaps you've put your focus on something you wanted to manifest, only to not really feel that happy or excited once it appears in your life. It could be that by the time you've manifested it you've already moved on and it's no longer a match for where you are now. But those anticlimactic feelings when your manifestations appear can often be the result of manifesting a dream that was never really *yours* to begin with.

We live in a world where we are constantly bombarded with images and ideas of what life should look like. Our friends and family influence us with their choices and opinions. TV, movies, music and other media influence us with their depictions of beauty, success and even happiness. And then there's social media …

There is a reason why they call popular social-media creators 'influencers'. Influencing is what happens when someone else's thoughts, beliefs, opinions and agenda affect and influence you to the point where you take on those thoughts, beliefs, opinions and agendas and they become your own.

When you're affected by other people's influence you can end up manifesting what they want, or what they want you to want. Most of the time this is all happening unconsciously, but when you do start to notice, you can become more discerning about where and when you're being influenced and make choices that are right for you.

Not all influence is negative, of course, and just as much as you can be negatively influenced towards wanting something that's not really in alignment with your own heart, you can also be positively influenced to live the life of your dreams. Finding people who support your dreams, media and social media accounts that inspire you, excite you and set your soul blazing are keys to helping you remember your heart's true desires.

GRAB YOUR JOURNAL!

- *Who are the people you most enjoy spending time with? How do they uplift and inspire you?*
- *List one to three TV shows, movies or books that inspire and uplift you.*
- *What accounts on social media inspire you to live your dreams?*

AWARENESS PRACTICE

Over the next 24 hours, get really curious about all the ways in which the outside world is trying to influence you. This isn't about judging yourself, this is just a process of noticing. We all get influenced and there's no shame in realising you've clicked on an ad for something you don't really want.

Just noticing is a positive and powerful step in returning to yourself. Notice when you see something you want – an item of clothing, a lifestyle or a state of being. Notice when you want what someone else has. Notice the many ways you're being advertised to in each moment. Notice when influencers are influencing you.

You'll very quickly start to notice when you're being influenced and with discernment decide if you want to accept it into your energy or not.

CLEARING AND PROTECTING YOUR ENERGY

Clearing and protecting your energy is another fantastic way to make sure that your desires are really your own. When you clear your energy you're essentially clearing away all the 'stuff' that isn't yours – the negative influence, other people's desires you've picked up, anything that isn't *yours*.

Protecting your energy is a powerful practice that can help stop you picking up anyone else's stuff in the first place. No one will be able to sell you something you don't really want, and instead of wanting what that person on social media has, you'll be drawn to accounts that inspire you to live *your* best life, even if it looks completely different to theirs.

TO CLEAR YOUR ENERGY

Clearing and protecting your energy is all about intention. There really is no wrong or right way to do it, but the following will help you get started.

You will need:

- *Aura mists, incense, ethically sourced sage or palo santo*
- *Salt water mixed into a spray bottle*

1. *Visualise a beam of white light moving down into the crown chakra at the top of your head and filling your entire body and aura with white light.*
2. *Clear yourself and your space with aura mists, incense, ethically sourced sage or palo santo smoke. A little salt water mixed into a spray bottle can also be spritzed around you.*

3. *Affirm* – I am clear. All aspects, expressions and extensions of me are clear in all directions of time and space. And so it is. *Say this three times every day.*

4. *Now fill yourself and the space with love, harmony, positivity and good vibes by visualising gold light or just calling in the energy you want through words and phrases.*

TO PROTECT YOUR ENERGY

- *Call on your guides, angels, ancestors or the Archangel Michael and ask for their protection.*
- *Visualise a shield of blue light all around you.*
- *Affirm* – I am protected. All aspects, expressions and extensions of me are protected in all directions of time and space. And so it is. *Say this three times every day.*
- *Set healthy loving boundaries with people.*

PRACTICES TO BREAK FREE OF NEGATIVE INFLUENCE

Here we'll look at how to identify where, when and how you are being influenced by others to want what they want, or what they want you to want, and provide some tips and tools for breaking free.

MEDIA

Some people on a spiritual or personal development path choose to completely avoid the media. They give away their TVs, never watch or engage with the news and try to avoid advertising as much as possible.

This is all great in theory, and if you choose to go down this path, power to you. For most of us, however, missing out on a new season of our favourite TV shows just isn't an option. Not all media is negative; in fact books, movies and TV shows can actually be incredibly inspiring and uplifting. They help us feel less alone and more understood, seen and connected. They tell stories of the light overcoming darkness and inspire us to be superheroes in our own ways. We get to experience life through other people's eyes as we gain more understanding, empathy and compassion. And who can resist a good love story with a happy ending? We've always loved to share and tell stories, we've been doing it for tens of thousands of years. It's a powerful way by which we can communicate and connect with each other.

We can break free of negative media influence when we become aware of the messages and motives behind the media we consume and become more conscious in choosing what we watch, read and listen to.

Remember, you don't need to watch what everyone else is watching and you don't need to like what everyone else likes. If you feel as if you're particularly sensitive to media influence and energy you might like to avoid watching anything too violent, gory, sexist or racist, but if you do find yourself wanting to watch a horror movie or something heavy, just visualise yourself surrounded with light. You can also visualise a thick pink light between you and the TV screen. Set the intention that you won't take on any of the energy in what you're watching. You can always cleanse yourself and the room afterwards, too!

Practice

Next time you're on your favourite streaming service, take a look at the movies and shows that are on your list. Remove anything that doesn't feel good, uplifting or inspiring (whatever that means to you!). Now put three to five new shows or movies on your list that look like they will positively influence and inspire you.

SOCIAL MEDIA

Many of us are beginning to become more aware of the issues surrounding social media. Never-ending scrolling feeds are not great for our nervous system: we are at the mercy of an AI algorithm to decide what we should and shouldn't see and there are more ads on these platforms than ever before.

But there is a positive side to socials, too. We can find our people, connect with inspirational and educational accounts and we can share our own light and inspire others through our own posts!

Again, it's all just about getting more conscious and seeing how and where social media is supporting you versus how it's negatively influencing you to want things that aren't really in alignment with your own heart.

Comparison is a double-edged sword; on the one hand it can make you feel bad about yourself – that you're not as pretty, smart, rich, successful or happy as someone else; on the other hand seeing people living their best lives can inspire us to do the same.

Practice

Go to your social media feed and notice how each post that comes up makes you feel.

Ask these questions:

- *How does this account make you feel?*
- *Do you feel like you need or want what they have? If so, why?*
- *Do you feel inspired or motivated?*

Unfollow or mute any accounts that make you feel like you're not enough as you are, and unfollow or mute any accounts that you feel are negatively influencing you. Then find and follow new accounts that feel inspiring to you!

FRIENDS AND FAMILY

Our friends and family don't usually negatively influence us on purpose. Often their opinions about how we should be living our lives come from them wanting the best for us. Sometimes they aren't. Some people like to control others out of their own ego stuff, in which case it can be a red flag to get some distance from that person if you can, or at the very least practise energy protection around them.

Again, one of the best things you can do when it comes to how you're influenced by your friends and family is to just notice. Go back in time and see if you can find a few ways in which your family and friends have influenced your path and your decisions both positively and negatively. How have they influenced your dreams, desires and goals? You don't need to go into blaming them or blaming yourself here, just notice and then release it. Whatever happened in the past can stay there. You get to make your own decisions moving forward.

GRAB YOUR JOURNAL!

- *How have your family members positively or negatively influenced your dreams and desires?*
- *How have your friends positively or negatively influenced your dreams and desires?*

FORGIVENESS

As you move into a deeper state of awareness around who and what's influencing you it can be useful to do some forgiveness work, not only towards those who may have negatively influenced you in the past, but also towards yourself for all the times you let someone or something else negatively influence you.

Forgiveness is a loving choice you make for yourself. Unforgiveness is heavy, it weighs on your heart and mind even when you're not thinking about it. To let it go is an act of self-love. You don't have to be okay with what anyone else did to you, but if you can find it in your heart to wish them well, or at least to let them go, it will clear space in your heart and mind and make you feel so much lighter.

And most of all, forgiveness creates space in your life for the good things to come in.

Forgiveness practice

Write letters to the people you want to forgive, release and let go. In your letter express all the pain and frustration – anything at all that comes up. End your letter with: *I send you love and let you go.* If that's too hard, try: *I wish you well and let you go.* And if even that's too much of a stretch, try: *I wish myself love and so I let you go!*

You can also write a letter to your past self who wasn't as discerning and aware as you are now and forgive them for anything they did or didn't do that you are still holding on to. Forgive yourself for the ways in which you were negatively influenced and set an intention to seek out inspiration over influence from here on out. And try to love yourself even if you do find yourself getting caught up in some influence that's not right for you. It's a journey, but every day you'll become more aware and awake to what's yours and what's not.

CANDLE MAGIC FOR RELEASING NEGATIVE INFLUENCE

This is a simple cleansing spell that can be used to help you clear yourself from any negative influence you've picked up. Use what you have, make it your own. It's all about intention.

You will need:

- *A white candle*
- *A candle holder and dish or a heatproof plate*
- *Small pieces of paper and a pencil*
- *Salt*
- *Sage, rosemary, peppermint or eucalyptus oil (optional)*
- *Matches or lighter*

- *A space outside where it's safe to burn candles and paper*

1. *Prepare your space outside and gather your tools.*
2. *Take a moment to centre your energy by taking a few deep breaths.*
3. *Visualise yourself filled with white light and affirm* I am clear *three times.*
4. *Visualise yourself surrounded by a blue shield of light and affirm* I am protected *three times.*
5. *Visualise roots of light growing into the earth beneath you and affirm* I am grounded *three times.*
6. *Call on the deities of your choice (see page 112 for more on deities). This could be an invocation to a specific guide or angel, your higher self, the goddess, god – whatever works for you. Just go with 'guides' if you aren't sure who to call. Call on them by saying:* I thank you [deity] for your love, presence, guidance and wisdom. Thank you for guiding my magic so that it may be done in alignment with my best and highest good.
7. *Take your candle and hold it to your heart. Say:* May this candle be a symbol of all the negative influence, thoughts, beliefs, opinions and desires I've picked up from others. As it burns down, may it burn away all that which is not mine from my mind, body, heart, energetic and auric fields.
8. *If you're using oil, dress the oil from the bottom of the candle upwards to direct the energy away from you.*
9. *Place the candle in the holder and sprinkle some salt anti-clockwise around the base of the holder or plate you're using.*
10. *On the pieces of paper, write down anything specific you know you've picked up and would like to release. You can also just write:* These are all the conscious and unconscious thoughts, beliefs and opinions I've picked up from others that no longer serve me.

11. *Take another deep breath and light your candle. Visualise it burning away anything that is not yours.*
12. *Take your time and burn each piece of paper you have written on. Collect the ash in the dish or plate under your candle.*
13. *Let the candle continue to burn down. If you need to pause the spell, use a snuffer to snuff out the candle, then re-light it once you're able.*
14. *When the candle has burned to the end, take the wax, ash and salt and put it in an outside bin or in the ground somewhere away from where you live.*
15. *Feel free, clear and ready to take on the world!*

POSITIVELY INFLUENCING AND INSPIRING YOURSELF

One of the simplest and most effective ways to positively influence yourself is through affirmations. Using affirmations is so easy and they really work! All you need to do is say them out loud or under your breath whenever and wherever you feel the need.

The rule of three works well for affirmations. Say them three times and finish with: *and so it is* another three times.

If you really want to etch a new positive thought or belief into your being, try using a mala. Malas have 108 beads and you can use them for prayer, mantras and affirmations. If you have a smaller bracelet mala or a rosary, this will work well too. Place your fingers on the starting bead, say the affirmation once, then move on to the next bead and say the affirmation again until you've completed all the beads on the mala.

Another great way to work with affirmations is to stand up, raise your arms and say your affirmations as loudly, clearly and confidently as you can. You may like to crank those high-vibe tunes while you do this.

You can also make songs out of your affirmations and sing them to yourself in the shower or the car.

Here are some affirmations to use to positively influence yourself and prepare yourself for manifestation:

I am clear of all negative influence and I am inspired, motivated and supported to manifest my heart's true desires.

I always manifest from my heart and live in love, purpose and joy.

I no longer take on any programming or influence from anyone or anything that is not in alignment with love.

Everything I manifest is in alignment with my heart's true desires.

I manifest my heart's desire with ease and grace.

GRAB YOUR JOURNAL!

Write down any of the above affirmations that resonate with you, then create some of your own.

Say them often, with power and intention!

INSPIRATION

Now it's time to get really inspired, lit up and excited about your life and what you're going to manifest. There's also an opportunity here for you to realise just how much you can inspire and uplift others!

GRAB YOUR JOURNAL!

- *Make a list of all the people, things, activities, experiences or places that inspire you.*
- *How can you engage with all these sources of inspiration often?*
- *How are you feeling called to inspire others?*

GETTING TO THE ROOT OF YOUR DESIRE

Essentially, this means figuring out the desire behind the desire. This really just involves questioning your desire over and over again until you figure out exactly what it is you want.

Here's an example. Say you want a better-paying job. Ask yourself why you want a better-paying job. The answer may be so that you can have some money left over after the bills are paid. Then you ask yourself *why* you want this extra money. Maybe you just want to feel more security in your life, then ask yourself *why* this is important to you. Continue this process of asking why until you reach the very root of your desire. In this example the root may be a simple desire to feel safer in the world. Doing this can help you see that there may be more than one way or one path to manifesting what it is you most want and need.

You can repeat this process for anything else you're wanting to manifest right now and come back to it for anything you want to manifest in the future.

GRAB YOUR JOURNAL!

Write down one thing you really want to manifest right now.

Work through the process above, asking why for each layer of your desire until you get to the root.

Now go through the following questions:

- *Why do you want this?*
- *What are you going to do when you have it?*
- *How is it going to change your life for the better?*
- *How is it going to change the lives of those around you for the better?*
- *How is it going to change the world for the better?*

QUICK-FIRE WHYS

In your journal, write down eleven things you want to manifest right now. Don't think about it too much, just write down the first eleven things that come into your head. They can be big or small, just list whatever you think of first.

When you're done, put your hand on your heart and take a deep breath. Now go through each thing you wrote and ask your heart if it's really in alignment for you.

Notice where you've written something that may be influenced by someone or something else in your life. Next to the things you want to manifest that feel good and aligned in your heart, draw a heart. Next to the things that feel like they've been inspired by someone else but still feel good, draw a star. Next to the things that feel like they might not be coming from your heart at all, draw a question mark.

Do this regularly as a way to check in to see if your desires are in alignment with your heart or coming from somewhere else.

THE EVOLUTION OF WHAT YOU WANT

We're always changing, growing and evolving. What you want in this moment may not seem so important to you in a few days, months or years. As you change and grow, so will your dreams and desires. Letting go of old dreams is an important part of the process. It's okay to change direction, to move towards something else. It's not failure to follow your heart into a new chapter.

GRAB YOUR JOURNAL!

Write down any dreams you've had for a long time. These may be about things you've wanted since you were a child – a dream house or a wedding you wanted when you were five years old – or they may be things you've wanted in more recent years.

Take some time to pause, hand on heart, and assess what you've written. Check in with your heart to see if you still want these things or if it's time to let them go.

Strike a line through anything you no longer want, any old dreams you are ready to let go of. Do this with intention, thank the old dreams for getting you to this point and then let them go.

When we let go of all the outer influence, the desires that aren't really ours and the old dreams that no longer resonate, we make space in our hearts and in our lives to call in the things we really do want to manifest in our lives.

WHEN YOU STILL DON'T KNOW WHAT YOU WANT

Work out what you *don't* want. When you know what *doesn't* fill your heart with joy, you're a little closer to knowing what will. Make a list of the things you no longer want in your life – work that doesn't fulfil you, friends who no longer support you, anything that's just not working in your life. Now take these and look at what they tell you – if you don't want to stay in a job that you don't love, maybe it's time to start manifesting work that really excites you. If your friends aren't there for you, it might be a sign to focus on manifesting some new people into your life.

Work on practising and developing your intuition. One simple way to do this is by taking some time to get quiet and still every day. Even just five minutes of meditating daily can help you connect deeper with your own heart. Close your eyes, take a few deep breaths and just sit, breathe and be with yourself.

Take a break from social media. Delete your apps for a weekend or put your phone on a high shelf. Too much scrolling is a really quick way to dull your intuition. Taking breaks can help you re-connect with your inner self and inner voice. Focus on simply manifesting clarity and a deeper connection to your intuition and heart. Manifest feelings and states of being instead of specifics. You might not know what you want, but you probably know how you want to feel!

In your practices and rituals, just ask for whatever is in alignment with your best and highest good. Your conscious mind may not always know what it wants, but there's a part of you that does. Get out of your own way and let that part lead you, even if you have no idea where you're going!

SPIRITUAL RETREAT FOR CLARITY

If you have the time and funds to go on an organised spiritual retreat, go for it. If you don't, no worries, you can create your own retreat and find just as much peace and clarity where you are.

You can do this in whatever way works for you and your lifestyle, but the idea is to plan a weekend, a day or even just an afternoon of spiritual goodness. No phone, no distractions, just you deepening your spiritual connection. Ideally, you'll do this retreat on your own, but if you have a friend who's doing this work with you, it could be fun to plan a retreat together!

Some ideas for your spiritual retreat:

- *Start the day with an early morning yoga and meditation session. Watch a recording of a class or do your own thing.*
- *Plan some delicious plant-based, nourishing and nutritious meals. Prep or cook them ahead of time or take time to cook your meals as part of your retreat.*
- *Make a picnic and plan a day of walks, adventures or just sitting in the park.*
- *Read your tarot or oracle cards.*
- *Journal on anything and everything.*
- *Read a spiritual book or listen to an inspiring audio book.*
- *Get arty and crafty. Make collages (see page 141 for how to make a vision board), paint, draw, knit, craft, mosaic or whatever your thing is.*
- *Meditate with guided meditations, sound bath or gong audios.*
- *Take a long salt bath.*
- *Chant mantras.*
- *Make malas, spiritual jewellery or friendship bracelets.*
- *Drink lots of herbal tea.*
- *Go somewhere you've never been before and take in the sights.*
- *Take a nap under a tree.*
- *Give yourself permission to rest and do absolutely nothing!*

Make the day or weekend yours and fill it with whatever makes your soul sing. Try to avoid other people, social media, even TV for at least one whole day and see how your energy shifts. You should start to feel clearer and may even get some deeper insights into what it is you really want to manifest in your life. Take your journal with you so you can jot down any guidance and ideas that come through.

CLEARING BLOCKS TO MANIFESTATION

In this section we're going to focus on clearing away anything that may be blocking your manifestations. These are the often small or unconscious things that prevent us from being able to call in, receive and then hold our dreams.

LIMITING BELIEFS

Your mindset is usually the place where you'll find the biggest blocks to being able to live your dream life. In the previous section we looked at the who, what and how of being influenced or taking on the ideas, beliefs, opinions, agendas and even dreams of others. In this section we're going to dive deeper and look at some of the common beliefs that get planted in our minds and stop us from being able to manifest our heart's desires. These beliefs usually come out of how other people speak to and treat us as well as how we speak to and treat ourselves. We can pick up these limiting beliefs from our family, friends, school and work, and also from comparing ourselves to others in the media or social media. They start off as little seeds, and as we go through life, and the more we believe and buy into them, the stronger and more set in they become. But as soon as we start to become consciously aware of them, it can be easy to begin to release and clear them.

Do any of these limiting beliefs sound familiar to you?

- *I'm not good enough.*
- *I don't deserve good things.*
- *Why should I get to live the life of my dreams?*
- *I'm not smart/pretty/talented/clever enough.*
- *Someone else deserves it more than me.*
- *I'm not special/interesting/unique.*
- *I'm too weird/awkward/no one gets me.*
- *I don't have anything to offer the world.*
- *I'll never be rich/successful/happy.*

Like the ego, limiting beliefs often try to keep us safe, but you can still feel safe and be discerning without limiting and hiding yourself and all you have to offer from the world.

Perhaps you find yourself about to take a leap of faith, applying for that dream job, booking a dream trip or going on a blind date, and suddenly you're thinking you're not good enough. It's in these moments that you always have two choices: you can listen to those limiting beliefs that tell you to stay home on the couch where it's comfortable, or you can take a chance, do something that may end in failure or could end in you scoring your dream job, taking the trip of a lifetime or meeting your soulmate!

GRAB YOUR JOURNAL!

- *Take some time to write down some of your own limiting beliefs.*
- *Pick three that feel the loudest to you right now.*
- *For each of them try to think about when this limiting belief was planted.*
- *Who or what makes you feel like this?*
- *How has this limiting belief affected your manifesting?*

LIMITLESS BELIEFS

Just like you did with positively influencing yourself in the previous chapter, you can also re-write your own limiting beliefs.

Go back to your journal where you wrote down those three main limiting beliefs and now re-write them into *limitless* beliefs. For example:

- *I am good enough.*
- *I deserve good things.*
- *We should all get to live the life of our dreams.*
- *I am smart/pretty/talented/clever enough.*
- *I am just as deserving as anyone else.*
- *I am special/interesting/unique.*
- *I embrace my weird and attract the people who get me.*

- *I have so much to offer the world.*
- *I can be rich/successful/happy.*

Write down any other limitless beliefs you'd like to anchor into your heart and mind.

As you go through your day, start noticing when limiting beliefs come up, and when they do, re-write them in your mind. You may like to imagine the belief being deleted with a backspace, being wiped off a board or just dissolving into light. You can also affirm: *cancel, clear, delete* or *I release this limiting belief now!* Then affirm out loud or in your mind the limitless version of that belief.

For example, as you're about to go on that blind date and you start to feel like there's no point because you're just not pretty or interesting enough, look yourself in the mirror and say: *I release this limiting belief,* then replace it with: *I am pretty enough, I am beautiful enough, I am absolutely fascinating, and I will find my soulmate tonight or very soon!*

It sounds corny, but this stuff really does work, and it's a lot easier than you think. All you need is the intention to make a change, and you will!

If you need an extra boost of magic, write your limitless beliefs on Post-it notes and stick them around your bathroom mirror, on the back of the toilet door, in your purse, car dashboard or anywhere you'll see them often. Write them on the inside of your wrist each morning. You can even abbreviate them or turn them into symbols or sigils (more about sigils on page 150) and only you will know your secret code. Every time you see that symbol you'll be reminded – you are good enough, you are beautiful, you are deserving of good things, and you do deserve to manifest your dreams!

WORTHINESS AND SELF-ESTEEM

Worthiness is such a huge block to manifesting for most people that even though we touched on it in the previous chapter it really deserves its own section.

Essentially, this is a self-love or self-esteem issue and it blocks so many beautiful, magical, wonderful people from living their dreams. People with the biggest hearts who have such capacity to do so much good for the world are often so caught up in worrying about or helping everyone else that by the time they find five minutes alone they have nothing left to give to themselves. When these gorgeous souls do have time for themselves, they often spend it worrying if they are doing enough or feeling guilty for not doing something else with their time. And when they do start to think about stepping into their power and sharing their truth with the world, they're often so worried about what others will think of them and how they will be judged that in the end it feels so much easier not to.

In spiritual truth we all know that we are beings of light having a human experience and that we are all just as worthy and wonderful as each other. We've just been so influenced to believe otherwise it can be hard to remember where our inner light switch is.

But some part of you does remember. Some part of you does believe that you can manifest your dreams and that it's okay for you to have everything you want – that's the part of you that knows you can do this and got you to this point in this book.

People who love themselves and feel worthy show up for themselves, just like you're doing right now. They do the work on themselves, they release the old and make way for the new. If you're here right now, know this: your heart's deepest truth is that you already do love yourself, you know you are worthy. You know with absolute certainty that you deserve a wonderful, happy, joyous and love-filled life. We just have to work together to release some of the junk that's in the way of you remembering that truth.

GRAB YOUR JOURNAL!

List all your self-love and self-care practices from cups of tea and long baths to giving yourself permission to rest and booking reiki or massage appointments.

Write down all the things you're already doing that prove you do love yourself and feel deserving and worthy of living the life of your dreams. This could include things like picking up this book, the ways in which you're working on yourself, the kind things you do for yourself and others and all the ways in which you're already showing up for your dreams, no matter how big or small.

JOURNEY TO THE PAST

This exercise is best done when you're somewhere quiet and can take some time to get into a meditative state.

Close your eyes and take a few deep breaths to centre your energy. Visualise a pink light in your heart opening up and expanding through your body and all around you, filling your aura. Then visualise a protective blue shield around you.

Take another deep breath, then think about one of the limiting beliefs you have that has been holding you back. Think of the first time, or another powerful memory where you felt that limiting belief was being formed. Don't take yourself anywhere too painful or traumatic, just think of a moment where this limiting belief was planted or began to grow.

Now take yourself *into* that moment. See yourself, now, looking on as this moment is happening. Notice how you feel, how the younger you in the scene is feeling, how anyone else present is feeling.

Approach this past version of yourself and tell them what you needed to hear in that moment. Tell them something that will make them feel better. Tell them not to take on this belief. Give them a warm hug and offer them anything else you feel will help them to release this and stay in their power. Give them a *limitless* belief to hold on to instead.

See this past version of you shining bright – smiling, happy, loved and empowered. Take yourself back into the present moment with three big deep breaths. Shake out your body and return, then write in your journal about what you experienced.

RELEASING GUILT

Guilt can be huge when it comes to blocks to manifesting. Perhaps you feel guilty about spending money on yourself, taking time to rest or doing something just for fun. It's human nature, at least for heart-centred humans like yourself, to feel deep empathy for those who have less than you do. This is natural and normal and not something you want to change about yourself. You don't want to get rid of your compassion, but you do want to release the guilt that blocks you from living your dream life and being able to shine your light even brighter in the world.

If you feel guilty for having more than others, it may be a sign that part of your dharma or purpose is to do something to help those you feel so much empathy for. When it comes to helping others the best way to do it is by reaching out a hand and lifting them up, not joining them in the depths – that only makes you both stuck.

Instead of feeling guilty for what you have, or for what you want, set an intention to help others when and where you can. Use the amazing life you are creating for yourself to help make a positive difference in people's lives. Give to charity, give your time, expertise and knowledge. Support causes you believe in, use *your* influence to positively help someone else.

GRAB YOUR JOURNAL!

- *What do you feel guilty for wanting or already having?*
- *What is this guilt teaching you about your purpose?*
- *Write down at least three ways by which you are going to help others once you have manifested your own dreams.*
- *Write down three things you can do right now to make a positive difference in the world.*

ENJOY YOURSELF RITUAL

Create a ritual around doing something you really enjoy but often feel guilty about. Maybe it's just taking time for yourself or staying in a nice hotel; whatever it is, set a date to do it with the full intention that you are not going to feel guilty.

Another wonderful way to curb guilt is to replace it with gratitude. As you are taking that time for yourself or having that weekend away, shift into gratitude. Every time you feel yourself slipping into guilt, say to yourself out loud or in your mind: *I am so grateful I can do this, I'm so grateful for this opportunity, I'm so grateful to be here right now*, or whatever other phrases of gratitude come to mind.

Never feel guilty for enjoying your life. When you fill your own cup it begins to overflow everywhere you go and you start to help and support others in ways you will never even realise.

COMPARISON AND COMPETITION

The jealousy that comes up when we want what someone else has can often be a key to discovering our own deeper desires and dharma. When you find yourself channelling the green-eyed monster, take a breath, put your hand on your heart and tune into your own intuition and guidance. Ask yourself if you really want what they have, or if there's something else at play here.

Working on being happy for someone else's success, rather than sitting in jealousy or judgement or thinking they don't deserve what they have, can help shift this energy and move you into alignment with your own success. If you feel triggered by someone else's success, happiness or situation, take time to sit with that feeling and unpack it, but if you can, reach out to that person and wish them well. Doing this can release the negative feelings you have, break the chains, raise your own vibe and move you more into alignment with what you do want.

Before I had my first book deal, I felt nauseous every time I saw someone else writing and publishing their books. I started commenting 'Congratulations!' and 'Well done!' on their posts, even when it was hard to do, but I eventually started to genuinely feel happy for them and, guess what? I eventually got my own book deal, too!

Wishing someone else abundance, prosperity and success is a major key in unlocking your own dreams.

JUDGEMENT

Judgement isn't always a bad thing. It can help us make snap decisions about others that keep us safe, it can help us to know if someone is going to be a good match for us energetically and if we should invite them into our hearts and homes. However, judging others for what they wear, how they spend their money or any other type of judgement can be an instant block to our own manifestations.

When you send out negative energy towards others it affects you more than it does them. When you judge another person, 99 per cent of the time it's about you, and not them. This also means when someone judges you, it's about *them*, not *you*, which is an empowering reminder! However, no one is perfect, and we all have moments where we judge someone else based on our own personal preferences and values.

You may disagree with someone's personal choices, but if they aren't harming anyone else it can be helpful to take some time to really sit with and unpack your judgements. The idea here is not to turn this into a self-judgement exercise – don't start judging yourself for judging others! Just get curious about where and when you go into judgement and why and begin to consider how it might be preventing you from living your own best life.

What we judge in others is what we block ourselves from receiving. If you notice you judge people who have money or judge their spending habits, you may find it more challenging to manifest money. If you find you judge other people's relationships, you may find it harder to have successful relationships yourself. Release your judgements of others and release your own blocks.

JUDGEMENT PRACTICE

You can do this practice in two ways. You can try to simply notice and get curious about when, where and why you judge people as you go through your day, or to make it a bit more fun you can turn on a reality TV show and sit with it for half an hour and notice how you judge people on the show. Those shows are great for this practice as they were created to trigger viewers' judgement!

When you find yourself judging someone either in real life or on the telly, ask yourself these questions:

- *How does this person make me feel?*
- *What am I judging them for?*
- *How could this judgement be blocking my own manifestation?*
- *How could I be more compassionate towards this person and their choices?*

MOVING INTO DISCERNMENT

As you work with this practice you should notice that you start to spend less time judging people and a little more time trying to understand them and sending them some love, or at the very least just being able to leave them to it.

Try to choose discernment over judgement. You still need to be able to work out who to trust and who to give your time and energy to. You still need to be able to avoid people and situations that aren't right for you. Instead of judgement, focus on being discerning, on trusting your intuitive nudges and following them.

When you're busy judging others, you're distracted. You're not focusing on creating your own amazing life. It's only when you can break free of the judgement and let others go their own way that you are truly free to go yours. Focus on your own magical lane ahead and you'll go much faster.

PAST LIFE BLOCKS

Not everything that holds you back from manifesting your dreams has been created in this life. We often carry ancient hurts, memories and vows from previous lives that affect us in ways we're completely unaware of.

If you're struggling to find an explanation for your limiting beliefs or find yourself repeating patterns or always coming up against the same blocks in your life but can't figure out why, it could be that you have some past life blocks to clear.

Past life issues can create energetic imprints within us that can block our manifesting even many lifetimes later. Some of the deepest imprints occur due to past life vows, and some of the most common past life vows we hold on to include:

- *Vows of chastity (making it difficult to attract, enjoy or keep romantic relationships).*
- *Vows of poverty (this can cause prosperity blocks).*
- *Vows of obedience or silence (often taken as religious vows that keep us small and quiet).*
- *Vows of protection (to protect someone or something with your life).*
- *Oaths to various causes, types of work or religions.*
- *Marriage vows (keeping you connected to a past life love).*

It can be helpful to get a past life reading or work with a past life regression meditation (these are available on my website), but there are also things you can do right now to begin to release these vows.

Just like going through a divorce to end a contract in the physical world, we can end these contracts energetically too. There is no reason to keep any of these vows. You're not the same person in this lifetime and you have a different purpose and path to walk now.

GRAB YOUR JOURNAL!

Think about any limiting beliefs, blocks or challenges you've had in your life that you think may be related to the above vows. Trust your intuition here.

As you read through this list, notice how your body reacts. Listen to the inner voice that will say yes or no to each one. You don't need to know who you were or what happened in a past life to be able to heal and release it. But on some level you do remember and you do know, so if anything comes up for you in reading this section, trust it. You may see an image of yourself in a certain place or time. Pay attention to that. Write it down, then write down any of the vows that could match with what you've experienced in your life so far.

RITUAL TO RELEASE PAST LIFE VOWS

This is a simple ritual you can do that will release any and all vows that you've made in past lives. You can do this anywhere, but you may like to create a sacred space and light a white candle before you begin.

Stand or sit up tall and raise your arms at sixty degrees, with your palms facing up and out.

Take a deep breath.

Say the following:

I now release any and all past life vows in all directions of time and space that no longer serve and support me on my soul's evolutionary journey. I release all vows of poverty, vows of chastity, vows of obedience, vows of silence and any other vows I have made in past lives that do not serve me now. I release all vows of marriage in all directions of time and space made with others that I no longer wish to be married to in this lifetime. I release all oaths I have made in past lives in all directions of time and space that are no longer in alignment with my beliefs, values and highest purpose in this lifetime. I am now free in this lifetime to forge a new path, choose my own destiny and live liberated from the past. And so it is. And so it is. And so it is.

ANCESTRAL BLOCKS

Another place where we've inherited manifesting blocks is through our blood and love lines. Our ancestral lines include our ancestral lineage by blood and by love (such as people who helped raise you who were not blood relatives, friends of the family, carers, and so on).

We inherit these blocks through the ways our parents and guardians spoke about and dealt with money, love, work – everything. But we also inherit them through energy imprints. You may never have met your great-grandmother, but you may still be carrying some of her manifesting blocks.

Your ancestors haven't gifted you these blocks, beliefs or stories on purpose; in fact, your ancestors really want you to enjoy your life. They don't want you to have to go through the difficult things they went through, they would much rather see you thriving and living the life of your dreams! This really is the best way to heal and clear ancestral blocks – to be happy, to enjoy everything this life has to offer. When you do this, you do it for your ancestors who weren't able to live as fully, freely and joyfully as you can. This creates huge healing for your ancestors, for you, and for all those who come after you. In fact, living a happy life really is the best way to clear your ancestral blocks.

MEDITATION TO CLEAR ANCESTRAL BLOCKS

Take a few moments to get yourself settled in a meditative state, then take a few big deep breaths and relax. Visualise a gold light pouring through the top of your head at your crown chakra and see it filling your body and aura with light. Visualise a blue light of protection all around you.

Take a few deep breaths now into your heart space. Visualise a beautiful pink, green and/or gold light here. Begin to open up the back of the heart and send a beam of light behind you, to all your ancestors, to all those who have come before you. See that light flowing through your ancestral lines, healing, clearing and sending love.

Now feel your ancestors stepping beside, behind and all around you. See or feel them opening up their hearts and pouring their love towards you. Let your ancestral line and yourself be healed, be held and feel their immense love for you. Just stay in this state for a little while, sending and receiving love.

Now open up the front of your heart chakra and send that beam of pink, green or gold light ahead of you, to all those who have come or will come after you. See yourself sending this love and light in both directions

– behind you and ahead of you. See yourself in the now moment, held and loved and supported by your ancestors while you all send love to the future together.

Take a moment now to just be and listen to any guidance that your ancestors wish to impart to you. This may come through as words, phrases, images or just a feeling or knowing.

When you feel that the work is complete, thank your ancestors for all they have done for you and continue to do for you. Come back into your body by taking three deep breaths, then take some time to integrate, rest and relax. Finally, write about your experience in your journal.

Now go forth and live your best life for your ancestors, yourself and all those who are yet to come.

FEARS

Sometimes it's just plain old-fashioned fear that steps in to block the path to our dreams. Fear goes both ways when it comes to manifesting. Sometimes it's the fear of things not turning out, of looking stupid, of trying and failing that prevents us from trying to manifest our dreams. But you may find that if you're really honest with yourself, you could also be a little afraid of getting everything you ever wanted.

Sometimes the fear of success is just as real as the fear of failure.

GRAB YOUR JOURNAL!

- *Write down one of the biggest dreams you have right now.*
- *Now make two lists: one for the fears you have around not being able to manifest this, on the other write down the fears you have about actually getting this thing.*
- *Spill it all. No one has to ever see this but you. Be honest with yourself and know you're strong enough to face all your fears.*

Now that you can see your fears all laid out in front of you, hopefully they don't seem so scary. Our fears, like judgement and the ego, are really just another self-preservation tool designed to keep us safe. There's nothing wrong with feeling fearful – fear is just a part of human nature – but when fear is blocking you from living your best life, it's no longer a useful survival tool.

Turn your journal a quarter way counter-clockwise and now write: *I thank and release these fears and let them go* all across those pages. If you like you can also rip them out and burn them in a sacred fire ceremony.

Fear will come up at different points on your journey and it's often a sign that you are growing, evolving and transforming. When fear shows up, ask what it wants to tell you, sit with it, feel it, thank it for its input, then let it go on its way.

BLOCKS TO RECEIVING

Sometimes our blocks occur later in the manifesting process. Have you ever been *this* close to getting what you wanted and then it fell through your hands? Maybe you'd been given an opportunity and a few days or weeks later it suddenly fell through, or maybe you had a great feeling that something was going to manifest and then … it didn't.

There are a number of reasons why this happens, but usually it's because on some level you're not ready, able or willing to receive your manifestation when it does show up. Sometimes the simplest reason for this is that you're just not used to receiving. Maybe it's not comfortable for you to receive gifts, help or kindness.

Do you ask for and accept help when you need it? Do you deflect compliments? When someone buys you a gift, how do you react? These can be clues to how open you are to receiving, and how you receive from others will mirror how you're able to receive your dreams.

A SIMPLE PRACTICE TO OPEN YOURSELF TO RECEIVING

When someone gives you a compliment, say thank you. Don't shrug it off, don't wave it away, don't talk yourself down. Don't respond immediately with a return compliment. Just say *thank you so much* and receive it with gratitude.

When someone offers to buy you lunch or a coffee or pay for something for you, say thank you and accept it. Don't push money in their face or get into an argument about who's going to pay. Just receive it with gratitude.

When you receive a gift of any kind – a physical item, a gift of time, energy, an act of kindness – express your gratitude and enjoy it! Practise receiving anything and everything good that comes your way, then it will become easier to receive everything you're trying to manifest.

MEDITATION TO PRACTISE RECEIVING

This practice is based on a Kundalini yoga meditation that is excellent for helping you to practise receiving.

With your palms facing up, bring them to touch, making a bowl shape with your hands at the heart centre. Close your eyes and imagine that everything you want is being poured into your hands. You might see white light, gold glitter or coins, or all sorts of goodness pouring in. If you find it difficult to visualise, just tune into the energy or intention of being open to receive. It doesn't matter what or how you see, feel or sense, just practise receiving.

Do this for 11 minutes, and as you do this meditation, notice what comes up for you.

GRAB YOUR JOURNAL!

Answer these questions in your journal:

- *What did you visualise, feel or sense was pouring into your hands?*
- *Where did it feel like it was coming from?*
- *Was it easy or difficult for you to practise receiving?*

If it was easy to receive for 11 minutes and this meditation had you feeling sparkly and excited about everything that's coming for you, great! However, if this felt challenging, keep practising. Try doing this meditation for just one to three minutes and build to a longer practice as it becomes easier.

GENERAL UNBLOCKING PRACTICES

These simple practices can be used to help you shift and unblock anything you're conscious or unconscious of and help clear the way for your dreams.

DECLUTTERING

Getting rid of physical items you no longer need and want can be deeply symbolic of a willingness to let go of the thoughts or beliefs, or the stuck, stagnant or negative energy that you no longer want in your life.

As you go about your decluttering practice, do it intentionally. Say to yourself as you go: *I'm releasing anything that blocks my manifestations. I'm making way for new wonderful things to come into my life.*

Donate anything that no longer has space in your life with the intention that it may bring blessings to someone else. Although this is a wonderful unblocking practice, it's also a way to keep the flow of prosperity moving in your life.

MOVING FURNITURE

The space you live in is an extension of you and your energy. When you move things in your home, you shift and wake up the energy of the space and also within you. Moving furniture around is a great way to shake things up and get them moving again energetically. Be mindful of where you move your furniture to. You might like to check out a book on Feng Shui or Vastu for some ideas about how to keep the flow of energy moving in your spaces.

FIRE CEREMONIES

Fire ceremonies are simple ways to release just about anything. If you specifically know what you want to release you can work with that, or you can perform a general fire ceremony if you're not sure what you need to let go of.

You can do these ceremonies with any type of fire – fire pit, fireplace, a candle in the garden. *(Note – always be careful with fire and never do a fire ceremony on a dry, windy day when there is potential for wild fires!)* Your ceremony can be as complex or simple as you like. You can take time to call on your guides and angels, prepare your energy, cast a circle, or you can just light the fire and sit quietly for a little while.

When you're ready, light your fire or candle. Write down what you want to release on small pieces of paper and throw them into the fire. A good idea is to sit with your paper and pencil and keep writing and letting go as new things come to mind.

As you throw your paper into the fire, watch it burn and know that it's burning and clearing out of your life. Take your time and enjoy this process. Sing mantras, sit and meditate, drink wine, do whatever feels good to you.

When you're done, safely put out the fire and say thank you to your guide and angels. Honour yourself by putting your hands on your heart, taking a deep breath and bowing to yourself.

OCEAN RITUAL

Similar to a fire ritual, this can be done with the energy of water. You can do this whenever you're at the beach, but you can also try it by a river, lake, stream – or even a small pond will do.

Pick up a pebble or any kind of stone and hold it in your right hand. Whisper into the stone what you would like to release, then throw it into the water with intention, releasing it to the water to wash away.

Clearing blocks to manifestation is a constant process. As you evolve, grow and work on manifesting different things you'll likely discover new blocks. The more you do this, the easier it will be to quickly identify what's blocking you and you'll be able to use the tools and practices above, or things you develop for yourself, to quickly release the block, break free and move forward.

Some blocks take years or even lifetimes to clear, but this doesn't mean you can't still manifest wonderful things in your life right now. Work with whatever blocks show up at the time. Don't worry about being completely free and liberated in every single area right now. Just focus on what's in front of you.

Also, try not to get so focused on what's blocking you that you forget to focus on manifesting your future. Notice when your blocks come up, do some work to release them but keep looking forward!

YOU HAVE THE POWER!

In this section you'll discover how to develop, deepen, call back and own your power. Connecting with your own power is like picking up a magic wand. When you believe in yourself, in your inherent inner divine power, in your ability to create the life of your dreams, nothing and no one can stop you!

THE POWER TO CHANGE YOURSELF AND YOUR LIFE

You really do have the power to create the life of your dreams, but remember that you can't change the world and you can't change other people, only yourself. That means that you can't make someone fall in love with you, you can't make anyone give you something that they don't freely want to give, and you can't take away anyone else's free will.

When you step into your power you don't get the ability to decide the fate of everyone around you, but you do get to decide yours. You can change how you interact with people, how you respond to challenges and how much light you radiate out into the world. You can change your own life, your own reality and your own story, but remember, everyone is on their own journey. Everyone is here to make their own choices, their own mistakes and walk their own path. Focus on yourself, on your path and on creating the most magical life for yourself. If it harms none, let other people go their own way.

CALLING BACK YOUR POWER

We've all given our power away at times, and on other occasions it's been taken from us with or without our permission. You give your power away when you say yes but you mean no, when you give so much of yourself to the point of exhaustion or whenever you find yourself in people-pleasing mode. You give your power away when you don't stand up for yourself or someone else, when you talk yourself down or whenever you just let life happen to you.

You may be giving your power away to someone or something right now; maybe you've given your power away in the recent past. You may have had your power taken away when you were a teenager or a child, and you may have given your power away in past lives, too.

GRAB YOUR JOURNAL!

- *Where or to whom are you giving your power away right now?*
- *Where have you given away your power in the past?*
- *When has your power been taken from you?*

Owning your true power is not an ego trip, it's not about always saying no or never putting someone else first, it's about healthy loving boundaries, knowing where you stand, honouring your truth and living with more confidence in who you are while still being loving and compassionate towards those you feel called to help and support.

A PRACTICE TO CALL BACK YOUR POWER

This is a simple practice and can be done as often as you feel you need to. No matter how good you get at holding on to your power there will always be times when you feel you want to call it all back to you.

Stand in the centre of a room (even a bathroom will do) and hold your arms out to the sides, palms up. State out loud: *I call my power back to me now. All the power that has been taken from me or given by me, willing or unwillingly, in all directions of time and space returns to me now.*

Say this three times, then finish with *And so it is* another three times. As you do this, visualise that all the lost pieces of your power are returning to you like golden puzzle pieces fitting back into your aura. See yourself shining bright, vibrant and whole. Then take a deep breath and know your power has been returned to you.

THE LAW OF ATTRACTION

We touched on the Law of Attraction in the Tough Stuff section of this book, and you may want to revisit that as we begin to work with these practices. Remember that not everything that happens in your life is the result of the Law of Attraction. Take responsibility where you need to, and let it go when it's not yours to carry.

The Law of Attraction is simply the idea that like attracts like, or cause and effect. You've probably already seen this play out in your own life many times. You have a good start to the day and your whole day seems to go pretty well, or you have a bad start to the day, one small thing goes wrong and suddenly your whole day is in chaos. This is like a snowball effect of the energy, thoughts and vibration you put out into the world.

When I worked in customer service, I was always much more likely to go above and beyond for customers who were polite and kind to me. And those who came at me with aggression or rudeness? I did the bare minimum that I could for them. So, try smiling at the universe and see what happens!

Working with the Law of Attraction is all about making yourself a magnet for what you want. Align your magnetic charge and soon people and opportunities will start to pick up on that charge and be drawn to you without even knowing why. Working with this energy allows you to not only work with specific dreams and desires and begin to draw them to you, but it also helps you to attract good things that you perhaps haven't even thought about it!

The other benefit of the Law of Attraction is that the better the energy you put out, the better you feel. Not only does the Law of Attraction work based on what you put out into the world, it also works on what you create within yourself. The more you send out love, compassion, purpose, peace and joy, the more you start to feel it expand within (and all around) you.

Look after yourself and your own energy as much as you can, but never blame yourself for attracting something 'bad' into your experience. Life happens, and this is a planet of duality. We came here to experience it all; working with the Law of Attraction is about vibrating in alignment with what you want as much as is humanly possible, and when things don't go to plan you'll have the ability, confidence and power to find solutions, lessons and ways through.

LAW OF ATTRACTION PRACTICES

The following simple practices will help you quickly see how working with the Law of Attraction can support your manifesting.

Smiling at strangers

This one can be tricky for introverts, but after getting out of your comfort zone the first few times it gets easier and even starts to become fun! Take a walk around your neighbourhood and smile at strangers. Catch their eye, give them a smile and see how they respond. Make a note of how many people smiled back at you compared to those that didn't. There will always be people who feel too self-conscious to smile back, or just shocked that a stranger is smiling at them, and don't know how to react, so don't take it to heart if they don't smile back. But when someone smiles back at you, notice how your smile has attracted that to you.

If you're not comfortable smiling at random people on the street, try smiling at the person who makes your coffee, shop assistants, people in your office that you don't know, and so on. You'll feel great and you might just make their day. Who knows, you may even make some new friends!

BECOMING WHAT YOU WANT TO ATTRACT

One of the most powerful ways to work with the Law of Attraction is to *become* what you want to attract. If like attracts like, there's no better way to get what you want than to *become* it! This is a little bit like faking it before you make it, but instead of faking it, you *become* it! No faking required!

Here are some examples:

- *If you want more love in your life, be more loving towards yourself and others.*
- *If you want someone to buy you flowers, buy yourself flowers.*
- *If you want more money, spend, save and invest the money you do have wisely.*
- *If you want a pay rise, walk into the office with confidence, knowing you deserve it.*
- *If you want more success, start owning your achievements.*

This is a really easy way to become a magnet for what you want, and it's a lot of fun, too. This practice can also help you build self-esteem, self-love and help you believe you are worthy.

GRAB YOUR JOURNAL!

- *What do you want to manifest in your relationships right now? How can you become this?*
- *What do you want to manifest in your work or career right now? How can you become this?*
- *What else do you want to manifest? How can you become this?*

ELEVATING AND EXPANDING YOUR AURA

Another way to start becoming a magnet that attracts all good things to you is to elevate and expand your aura. The aura is the energetic extension of you that expands out around your physical body. Your aura may be quite small, just a couple of inches thick, or it can extend to many feet wide. A healthy aura is about arm's length around you. Take a moment to hold your arms out to the sides, then visualise your aura shining like a bright light all around you.

A weak aura is small and can also have holes or tears. This usually occurs when someone is fearful, doesn't want to be seen or noticed, has been hurt by others or is having difficulty owning their power. You can expand your aura quite far when you need or want to, and it can be useful at times when you need to speak in a meeting or to a large crowd, but it's not always a positive thing to have the biggest aura in the room.

People who have massive auras can be trying to manipulate and control people in their field or may be overstretching themselves, taking on too much and literally being pulled in all directions. So, aim to expand your aura to arm's-length aura – this is plenty big enough to attract to you everything you desire.

The colour of your aura can change often and may include many different colours.

Here's a quick start guide to aura colours:

- *Blue – calm, peaceful, purposeful.*
- *Indigo – intuitive, spiritual.*
- *Green – growth, love, healing, abundance.*
- *Ruby red – passion, energy, confidence.*
- *Dark red – anger, rage, aggression.*
- *Yellow – powerful, happy, joyful.*
- *Orange – creative, energised.*
- *Pink – love, romance, playfulness.*
- *Purple – spiritual, connected, wisdom.*
- *Black/Grey – disconnected from the heart, in need of support.*
- *White – elevated, clear.*
- *Gold – very high-vibrational, prosperity, wealth.*

AURA PRACTICE

Close your eyes, take a few deep breaths and visualise your aura right now. Don't judge or worry that you're not doing it right, just let yourself see or feel what comes up. Notice how big or small your aura feels, see if you get any visuals, thoughts or senses of the colour of your aura.

Now see if you can expand your aura to that arm's distance all around you. Visualise your aura as a bright light all around you in a beautiful colour that feels perfect for you in this moment. If you notice any holes or tears in your aura, see this light filling those spaces and becoming whole again. Now see your aura shining a beautiful gold colour, expanded all around you and glowing beautifully.

When you're ready, open your eyes again and notice how you feel. Write about your experience in your journal.

Keep checking in with your aura daily and notice if it changes colour or size, then visualise it expanded and bright all around you.

MANIFESTING WITH YOUR AURA

As your aura becomes stronger and more vibrant you can begin to use it as a magnet to draw your dreams to you. You can think of the aura like a beacon of light, sending out a frequency that is in alignment with what you desire.

Think about something you want to manifest. What kind of aura do you think you will need to have to be able to attract it? For example, if you want to manifest a high-vibrational romantic partner you might want a pink and/or gold aura, or if you want to bring in success at work perhaps you'd choose bright ruby red, yellow or orange. For money, you might want to go with a bright gold. If you just want to bring more peace into your life a blue aura may help you attract and create it.

Get into a meditative state by taking a few deep breaths and relaxing for a few moments. Place your hand on your heart and visualise the colour you want your aura to hold. Begin to see your heart pulsing out that light and filling your aura. See your aura growing bright and strong all around you.

As you do this, hold the intention for what it is that you're wanting to manifest. State out loud or in your head: *My aura is the perfect vibrational match with [whatever you want to manifest] and it attracts this to me now.*

Say this three times and finish with: *And so it is, and so it is, and so it is.*

This is a simple practice you can do anywhere and at any time. You can close your eyes on the bus and do it, do it while you're lying in bed, whatever works for you! The stronger your aura is, the easier it is to attract to you what you want and hold it once it arrives.

MANIFESTING YOUR HIGHEST DESTINY

In the Kundalini yoga tradition there's a concept called the Highest Destiny. This is like the highest potential or the best and highest life you are able to live in this lifetime.

We all have a trajectory that is available to us when we're born, but most people never realise they have a choice as to how high they can rise on that trajectory. Most of us start out on the 'fate' level, which is where you are when you live your life passively, going about your day, letting life happen to you and not thinking too much about who you are or why you're here. When you're living in this state and something good manifests in your life you might call it fate or luck, you usually wouldn't contribute it to your own thoughts, energy or actions. When challenges come up on the fate path it's easy to blame someone else, life, god or the universe for your problems. If you're reading this, you can be pretty sure you're no longer walking the fate path.

Living your highest destiny is like reaching your full potential in this lifetime. It's not about perfection or reaching some unachievable way of being, this is about you feeling the best you can, living your purpose, making a positive difference to the lives of others (and to yourself!) and enjoying yourself in the process.

When you live in alignment with your highest destiny, you're on a kind of accelerated spiritual programme. You learn lessons more quickly and easily and you use them to ride the highest wave possible for you in each moment. You own your power on the destiny path and life gets easier, has more meaning and becomes so much more abundant and prosperous. And when you align to your highest destiny, you're able to manifest everything you need to live it.

GRAB YOUR JOURNAL!

- *Are you living in fate (letting things happen to you) or destiny (working on creating your best and highest life)?*
- *What does living your highest destiny mean to you?*
- *What would it look like if you reached your full potential in this life?*
- *What needs to change right now so you can start to live your highest destiny?*

INVOCATION

Try saying this invocation every day. You can do this at your altar, on your yoga mat, in bed, in the shower or on your commute. Just be sure to say it daily and see what difference it makes in your life.

> Thank you [universe/guides/angels/higher self, whoever you want to call on] for helping me to walk my best and highest path. Thank you for helping me to live my best and highest life. Thank you for helping me to reach my highest destiny in this lifetime. And so it is.

ALIGN YOUR CHAKRAS TO ALIGN YOUR LIFE

Getting your chakras aligned is like aligning your life from the inside out. The chakras are the energy centres of the body, they connect the physical body with the energy body, kind of like big buttons of light holding our energy bodies into place.

A great way to start to feel more aligned to your heart, your dreams and the life you really want to live is to work on aligning your chakras. Although each chakra has a different energy, they all work as one column and when they are lit up and aligned, so are you!

When something is causing concern in the physical body in the location of a chakra, it can be a sign that your energy needs aligning, but please always see a healthcare professional if you're having any physical issues.

THE CHAKRAS IN A NUTSHELL

- *Earth star chakra: Sitting in the Earth below your feet and physical body, this chakra is dark green or earthy toned and connects you to the Earth and the ancestors.*
- *Root chakra: This chakra sits at the base of your spine, is ruby red in colour and represents your material needs, work, money and security.*
- *Sacral chakra: Sitting in the belly, this chakra is orange and represents creativity, relationships and intuition.*
- *Solar plexus chakra: This chakra is located between the belly and the heart (right at the solar plexus) and is bright yellow in colour. This is the chakra of personal power and confidence.*
- *Heart chakra: Sitting right at the heart, this chakra is green or pink in colour and represents love in all forms, both giving and receiving.*
- *Throat chakra: Located at the throat, this chakra is blue and represents clear communication, truth and self-expression.*
- *Third eye: This chakra sits between and slightly above the brows, is indigo in colour and connects you to your psychic awareness.*
- *Crown chakra: Sitting at the top of the head, this chakra is purple or violet in colour and represents wisdom and knowledge.*
- *Causal chakra: Sitting just above and slightly behind the head, this chakra is silver in colour and looks like your own personal moon halo. It connects you to your guides and angels and to the cycles and flow of your life.*
- *Soul star chakra: Right above your head at the top of your aura and shining a bright gold colour, the soul star connects you to your soul, higher self and purpose.*

CHAKRA ALIGNMENT MEDITATION

Working with the chakras could easily be an entire book, but here is a quick and easy way to begin to align your chakras. This meditation is available to download for free from my website, or you may like to record this meditation in your own voice and listen back to it. You can have a friend read it for you, or just read each section at a time, closing your eyes between each section as you relax and visualise at each chakra point. You can do this meditation as often as you like. If you feel out of sorts do it daily until you feel more aligned again.

Take a few deep breaths and begin to relax. Visualise yourself letting go of anything that's not yours, any negativity or any stress or tension you're holding on to. Take a deep breath. Send your awareness to the earth star chakra below your feet. See this chakra shining and spinning an earthy deep green colour. Feel yourself connected to the Earth, to nature, to the plants and animals and all those who've walked the Earth before you. Give thanks to the Earth, to goddess Gaia, mother nature. Send love from your heart down into this chakra that sits in the Earth and see it radiating down and through the entire Earth beneath you.

Bring your awareness up now to your root chakra at the base of your spine. See this chakra shining and spinning a bright ruby red. Feel yourself connected to the material world. As you focus on this chakra give thanks for your home, your work, the money in your bank account. Feel deeply held and supported here, trust and know that all your material needs will always be met. See any worry or fear over your material needs burned up by this radiant red light. Trust and know you have everything you need and will always be safe.

Now send your awareness into the sacral chakra in your belly. See this chakra shining and spinning a bright radiant orange. Feel the creative flow being activated here as you move into deeper trust in your ability to create the life of your dreams. Feel any creative blocks being cleared as you move into flow.

Move up to the solar plexus chakra and see this chakra shining and spinning a bright yellow light. Feel your inner personal power waking up now. Know that you can stand in your power, ask for what you want and make it happen. You have the power. See any fear of stepping into your power being burned away and transmuted by this yellow light. Trust that it is safe to stand in your power, to take up space and to lead with love.

Send your awareness up to the heart chakra. See your heart glowing, shining and spinning a beautiful pink and green light. Let your heart open up and send love to all the people in your life, to all areas of your life, and let yourself feel a deep sense of self-love here. Feel the love from the universe filling your heart to overflowing. It is easy for you to love and to receive love.

Move up to the throat chakra now. See your throat shining and spinning as a bright blue light. Feel your throat opening and expanding, any constriction or fear of speaking your loving truth is being cleared, transmuted and healed. It is safe for you to speak your truth. It is time for you to communicate your desires, to ask for what you want and want to receive.

Send your awareness up now to the third eye chakra between and slightly above the brows. See a shining and spinning indigo light here as well as a physical eye opening up in the centre of your forehead. Let your awareness open up and expand. It is safe for you to see with your spiritual sight. Intend that you will only ever see loving and helpful images with your third eye. See your third eye opening up to spiritual truths and deeper love and awareness.

Now move up to the crown chakra at the very top of your head. See this chakra shining and spinning a light purple colour. As this chakra spins and activates, feel yourself opening up to the wisdom and guidance from your guides, angels and other beings of light. Trust that this wisdom will guide you safely on your highest journey.

Send your awareness now slightly above and behind your crown to the causal chakra. See this chakra shining and spinning in silver, opening up your psychic connection and spiritual power.

Connect now with the soul star chakra that floats above the physical body, just above your head. See this chakra shining and spinning a beautiful bright gold. Feel yourself connecting deeply to your own soul, your higher self. Remember that you are a being of light having a physical experience and that the truth of who you are always knows the best next step, the path of your highest destiny. Feel yourself filled with the light of your own soul and follow that path. Take some time here to pause, rest and integrate everything you've just experienced.

When you feel ready to come back, take three deep breaths, rub your feet on the floor, rub your palms together, and very slowly and gently come back into the room and open your eyes.

YOUR EMOTIONAL GUIDANCE SYSTEM

Your emotions are a powerful guidance system and they are often trying to guide you towards your best and highest good, whether you realise it or not. You may prefer to avoid the tough emotions, but even those are guiding you towards something better. When you feel miserable, frustrated or angry at a certain situation it's a pretty big sign that something isn't working. Again, this isn't about avoiding the tough emotions, it's about recognising the power behind them and using them to direct your sails, to propel you towards something that feels better.

When heavy emotions do come up, ask yourself:

- *What is this emotion trying to tell me?*
- *What is this feeling guiding me towards or away from?*

It's not only the tough emotions that can guide us either. When you feel joy, love, peace, harmony, light, ease or gratitude, pay attention to what's going on during these times. These are guideposts to the things that your heart and soul want more of!

When light emotions come up, ask yourself again:

- *What is this emotion telling me?*
- *What direction is this emotion guiding me towards?*

We're constantly experiencing different emotional states although we don't always pay that much attention to them. It's not always socially acceptable to show our emotions, whether it's crying at work out of frustration or skipping along the beach out of pure joy. But paying attention to how you are feeling will help you to be much more tuned into your own inner guidance and to know which path really is the path of your dreams so you can manifest it!

CHECKING IN WITH YOUR EMOTIONS

Take some time each day – in the morning and at night is ideal to start – to write down how you're feeling. This doesn't have to be something that takes very long, just a few words can be useful. You may also like to jot down what caused that emotional state, such as an argument with your boss, meeting up with a friend, reading a good book, and so on.

It seems basic, but we are so wired to feel 'fine' all the time that it can be a powerful activity to give yourself complete permission to feel your feelings and start to see them as a powerful guidance system leading you back home to yourself.

As you work through the practices in this book, including meditating and raising your vibration, you should start to notice that your emotional state improves and that you start feeling better about yourself, more empowered to let go of things you can't change and to make positive changes where you can.

THE POWER OF YOUR WORDS

Words have incredible power, and whether you're aware of it or not, you're manifesting every time you open your mouth to speak, send a text or post, or comment on social media. Watching your words isn't about lying or saying things that aren't true, it's not about never being allowed to vent or rant or complain again, it's about being conscious of when, where, how and to whom you do it.

Watching our words is often fascinating at first because we usually have no idea just how much we're belittling ourselves, reaffirming things that we don't want or judging others.

Here are simple ways to start using the power of your words:

- *Watch how you talk about what you want to manifest. For example, if you want to manifest money, try not to talk about how broke you are. You can flip the script by saying things like,* I don't have the money for that just now, *or* I'm choosing not to spend my money on that.
- *Notice how you speak about yourself, and instead of berating yourself for failing at something, congratulate yourself for showing up!*
- *Practise your self-talk by talking to others. Tell other people how fantastic you think they are and it should start getting easier to use that language with yourself too.*
- *When you notice yourself judging someone, try to see the good in them. Instead of gossiping about what someone else is wearing, mention how confident they are or how it's great they just express themselves in that way.*
- *Only comment positively on social media and avoid debates that are only going to bring you down.*

ASKING FOR WHAT YOU WANT

Whether you're asking the universe, your higher self or someone in the physical world who you can help you, there really is no right or wrong way to ask for what you want, but here are a few tips to help you make your intention clear as you begin putting it out into the universe:

- *Be succinct – Use as few words as possible to not only make your intention clear, but so you can remember it, write it, use it as an affirmation and hold the vision for it.*
- *Be specific – The more specific you can be, the better. Don't just ask for a new job, ask for a job that will really fulfil you, that's close to home, that has opportunities for promotion.*
- *But don't be too specific – Focusing your intention on manifesting a specific job at a specific company, for example, may mean that you end up missing out on your dream job just around the corner at a company you've never heard of.*
- *Stay open-minded – Always ask for this or something better and be open to receiving blessings that haven't even crossed your mind.*

HELPERS IN THE SPIRIT REALM

We talked at the beginning of this book about the importance of having a connection to the divine, whatever that means for you, and now we're going to look at some specific ways you can call on even more helpers in the spirit realm.

There are so many beings of love and light out there ready, willing and able to come and support you in manifesting your dreams. To call on your helpers in the spirit realms all you really have to do is ask them for their help. It's as simple as saying right now: *Dear helpers in the Spirit Realm, please support me on my journey of manifesting my dreams.* See them as your new best friends. You can talk to them about what you want, ask for their help in getting it, let them show you your next steps, help you clear any blocks and help you with your mindset. Many of them can also move through both the physical and energetic world to help shift, prepare and align things on your behalf.

Remember, this is a relationship like any other. Don't make it too one-sided; always thank them for their help. You may like to set up an altar or light a candle for them as a way to thank them for their support. Your spirit helpers are not here to do your bidding, they are here to support you because they want to see you happy and thriving and help you do all the wonderful things you are here to do in this life.

SPIRIT GUIDES

Your spirit guides, or just guides (a term that is often used for any of the beings who are with you), can be any being in spirit who has your back. Spirit guides are usually people who've lived good and often spiritual lives on Earth, and they now want to support others. Spirit guides are often most concerned with your spiritual path, so they may not help you manifest that new pair of shoes (unless they are going to have a positive impact on your spiritual journey), but they can help you with finding the right job, home, relationships and spiritual teachings and teachers.

ANGELS

Angelic beings are wonderful to work with for manifestation as they will always help you to manifest from the heart, soul and higher planes. If you call on the angels for support you will rarely have to worry about manifesting the wrong thing as they will always guide you to the highest outcome. The angels are completely nondenominational and show up in many religions and spiritual paths. They are happy to work with and support anyone who calls on them.

Angels for manifestation

- *Archangel Uriel – he will help you bring your ideas into physical form.*
- *Archangel Sandalphon – the archangel of answered prayers, he can help your prayers be heard and answered.*
- *Archangel Gabriel – this angel can help you manifest self-expression, aligned work and being seen and heard in the world.*
- *Archangel Ariel – a great angel to call on for support in manifesting your material needs.*
- *Archangel Michael – if you need help figuring out what you want, this angel can help you get clear and aligned with your vision.*

ANCESTORS

Your ancestors are wonderful helpers when it comes to manifesting anything to do with family, relationships and home life. They also want to see you comfortable and well looked after, so call on them when you need your material needs met.

GODS, GODDESSES, SAINTS, ASCENDED MASTERS AND OTHER DEITIES

There are many deities you can call on to help you manifest your dreams. Again, although these beings are associated with certain religions or spiritual paths, they are all happy to work with anyone who has good intentions.

Some powerful deities for manifestation include:

- *Morgan le Fay – a powerful goddess from Arthurian legend who can help you with your magic, witchcraft and stepping into your power.*

- *Merlin – one of the ultimate allies for magic and manifestation work!*
- *Goddess Fortuna – the ancient Roman goddess of fortune can help turn things in your favour.*
- *Goddess Aphrodite – the ancient Greek goddess of love can help you to manifest more love and romance into your life.*
- *Goddess Vesta – the ancient Roman goddess of home and hearth can help you with manifesting a new home or better home life.*
- *Goddess Lakshmi – the Hindu goddess of prosperity can support you with manifesting money and material needs.*
- *Lord Ganesha – the Hindu god of removing obstacles can help you with busting blocks and clearing the way for your manifestations to come to you.*
- *Quan Yin – as a goddess of mercy she will make sure you only manifest what is truly in alignment with your heart's desires.*

HIGHER SELF

Your higher self is like the soul aspect of you, the part of you that remembers your past lives, knows your highest destiny and guides you towards it. You are probably already more tuned into your higher self than you realise, as it is, after all, just an extension of you.

A wonderful way to start to work with your higher self is with this affirmation: *I am my higher self.* Every time you say this you are anchoring a little more of your soul energy into your own heart and mind.

ELEMENTALS

You may know the elementals as faeries, mermaids, gnomes, sprites, nature spirits or various other names. Elementals are known to help humans with manifestation, although they may want something in return for helping you. Usually this is just some recognition, a word of thanks, gifts of crystals or food items, but you can also show your gratitude by picking up rubbish you see in nature and by looking at ways to minimise your own environmental footprint.

Elementals, unlike spirit guides, angels, ancestors and other deities, are still connected to ego, which means they can choose whether or not to help you and often also have their own agendas. If you would like to work with the elementals, always be very respectful and trust your intuition. If the connection you make with an elemental being feels loving and helpful, go for it. If anything doesn't feel right, say thanks and let them know you've decided not to accept their help.

Elementals are nature spirits, so it can be especially helpful to call on the fae, gnomes or spirits of the land you are on or the land you are wanting to live on if you are looking for a new home. Ask them to guide you to the land and home that is energetically a good match for you. You can also call on them for anything else you need relating to nature.

The mermaids are powerful allies when doing shadow work or diving deep into your own subconscious to clear, heal and release anything that no longer serves and supports you.

BELIEVING IN YOURSELF

We've talked about believing in a higher power, spirit guides and angels, but if you really want to manifest your dreams you also have to believe in yourself.

This can take time, and it's not like you can just flip a switch after years, maybe even decades of *not* believing in yourself. But now is the time to start. Today is the day you get to start rewriting the story and reconnecting with your own awesomeness.

You are incredible. You are powerful.

It's time to break free and tell the world and the universe that you're ready to see the truth of your own greatness, to own it and use it to create a fantastic life for yourself and make the world a better place in the process.

So say it with me now:

I believe in myself. I believe in myself. I believe in myself.

Say it as often as you need to. Make it your mantra. Say it to yourself at night while you're drifting off to sleep and first thing in the morning. Look at your reflection in the mirror, in bus and shop windows, and say: *I believe in you.*

Successful, happy people believe in themselves. They know they can do it.

Know that you can do it, too.

BELIEVING IN YOUR DREAMS

Manifesting your dreams requires belief in those dreams. If you're trying to manifest huge sums of money but don't *really* believe that it will happen, it's a lot less likely to manifest.

Start by manifesting things you really believe could happen and come into your life. If a huge sum of money seems impossible to manifest right now, start with something smaller, like a raise at work, a better-paying job or a cheaper (and even nicer!) place to live.

Manifesting works really well when you focus on what's just out of reach but still believable and achievable. You can keep putting your bigger dreams out into the universe as well, but in your practices and rituals, focus on calling in the things you can really believe, and imagine it can happen for you here and now, or very soon.

As you gain more confidence with your manifesting, belief in yourself and ability to make things happen, you can start dreaming even bigger!

MANIFESTING FOR OTHERS AND THE WORLD

As you step into your power and start manifesting wonderful things, you may find that your desire to do more for others and the world grows. When you're no longer so focused on your own survival and you feel more abundant, supported and purposeful in your life, of course you are going to want to extend that out to others. A good way to start to do this is to think about how what you are manifesting can not only support you but also help others and the world around you.

Perhaps you want to manifest work opportunities where you're able to have a bigger positive impact on the lives of others, or to manifest enough money for yourself that you can support ethical companies and give more money to charity. Maybe you want to manifest more time to spend with your family or helping out in the community.

Step into your power, live your best life and inspire and support others to do the same.

PART THREE

MAKING IT HAPPEN

THE BEST TIMES TO MANIFEST

The best time to do your manifesting rituals and practices is whenever it feels right for you. If you get the nudge or feel excited to do some manifesting work, that's the perfect moment! But if you do want to add a little extra oomph to your magic, the following are traditionally known to be the best times for manifestation work.

DAYS OF THE WEEK

- *Sunday – best for manifesting with divine helpers and working on your spiritual development.*
- *Monday – connect with your intuition to get clear on what you want.*
- *Tuesday – a good day for taking action.*
- *Wednesday – best for expressing your desires to the universe in words or writing.*
- *Thursday – excellent day for general manifestation, especially work, money and the material world.*
- *Friday – great day for all manifestation, especially love and relationships.*
- *Saturday – wonderful for all manifestation, especially great for goal-setting and planning how you're going to make it happen. Also a great day for releasing manifestation blocks.*

TIMES OF DAY

- *Ambrosial hours – the early hours just before dawn are often considered the most powerful for any kind of spiritual work. It's usually quiet (you're probably the only one awake), you're still in a relaxed and rested state and haven't been influenced by the world around you yet.*
- *First thing in the morning – if you can't get up before sunrise, first thing in the morning is also a good time to manifest.*
- *Sunset – a good time for gratitude and releasing.*
- *The witching hour – late at night when everyone else is asleep is also a good time to manifest. As with the early hours, you can usually find a quiet place to connect with your own heart, desires and divine helpers.*

MOON CYCLES

- *Dark Moon – a time for deep inner reflection and considering what you most want to manifest.*
- *New Moon – an excellent time for all manifestation work.*
- *Waxing Moon – when the moon is 'growing' it's a great time to keep watering the seeds you've already planted. Also good for new manifestation work.*
- *Full Moon – good for manifesting but best for gratitude and releasing.*
- *Waning Moon – great for continuing to release blocks and all that no longer serves you.*

TIMES OF THE YEAR

All of the sabbats are powerful days for manifestation:

- *Samhain (Halloween) – honour those who've come before and manifest with the ancestors.*
- *Yule (winter solstice) – practise receiving. Manifest with candle magic.*
- *Imbolc – work with fire ceremonies and create manifestation altars.*
- *Ostara (spring equinox) – plant new seeds. A great time for all manifestation work.*
- *Beltane – powerful portal day for all manifestation.*
- *Litha (summer solstice) – great for manifesting abundance and prosperity.*
- *Lammas/Lughnasadh – practise gratitude and manifest what will serve you, others and the collective.*
- *Mabon (autumn equinox) – focus on gratitude, releasing, and both giving and receiving.*

OTHER POWERFUL PORTAL DAYS

LION'S GATE

The Lion's Gate occurs on the 8 August (8/8) every year when the Sirius star aligns with the Earth and the sun. This alignment is said to have been honoured by the ancient Egyptians and has become popular with modern witches and spiritual seekers. This energy alignment brings a potent opportunity to walk through the Lion's Gate portal, releasing the old self and becoming more aligned to the truth of who you really are. This is a time when big dreams can be put into motion.

A few weeks before this alignment, begin to think about what you most want to manifest in your life. Get very clear on what that is and then use the Lion's Gate to help you make it happen.

1111 PORTAL

Another very high-vibrational day to manifest is on 11 November (11/11). In numerology one represents new beginnings, personal power and manifestation; eleven is a master number in numerology that holds a powerful spiritual connection and energy. When we have four ones (1111) that manifestation power expands and creates a very special day for manifesting.

Think of the two elevens as pillars of light and visualise yourself walking through them into the life of your dreams.

NEW YEAR'S EVE/NEW YEAR'S DAY

This is one of the most powerful manifesting portals of the year. The collective buzz around setting resolutions, intentions and making wishes amps up the energy big time! Use this extra energy to let go of what you want to leave behind you and to manifest what you want for the year ahead.

BIRTHDAYS

Another fantastic time for manifesting is on or around your own birthday. As you complete another trip around the sun it's the perfect time to check in with where you are on your path, let go of old versions of yourself and set intentions for what you want to create in the year ahead.

TIMES TO AVOID

While you absolutely can manifest whenever you like, there are some times when you may find it more challenging than others.

RETROGRADES

You can still manifest during a retrograde, but you may find it takes longer or comes with extra learning opportunities and growth. Retrogrades are generally a good time to reflect on what you've already manifested, to check in with where you are and consider what you want to focus on next. It's not a time to force or push anything to happen.

Retrograde cheat sheet:

- *Mercury* – communication, logic and intellect.*
- *Venus – love, relationships and pleasure.*
- *Mars – energy, action and passion.*
- *Jupiter – luck, expansion and growth.*
- *Saturn – structure, responsibility and leadership.*
- *Uranus – individuality, liberation and inspiration.*
- *Neptune – imagination, dreams and spirituality.*
- *Pluto – transformation, death and rebirth.*

* During Mercury Retrograde pay extra attention to how you communicate your desires to the universe.

ECLIPSES

Eclipses are very chaotic energy and it's not advisable to do manifesting rituals at these times.

GATHERING MAGICAL SUPPLIES

In this section you'll find a list of items that can enhance your manifestation practices. None of these are essential and you can always just use what you have on hand. For centuries wise folk have been working their folk magic with whatever was available to them, and your magic will be just as powerful as long as you work with the right intention.

Working with magical items in manifestation or any kind of magic and witchcraft is really just a way to weave spiritual energy and intention into the material world. As you take a herb or oil and dress a candle or anoint an object you are moving your intention into the physical. You are creating a physical change in the world to begin the process of the bigger change you want to see taking place. Just like writing down an idea or sharing it with someone can make it seem more real, as you work with magical tools you place your ideas, dreams and wishes into objects like anchor points into the material world.

Working with tools is a way to commit to your intentions, like gathering and mixing the ingredients for the cookies of your dreams!

A note on ethics

Not all magical tools are created or sourced equally. Take some time to do your research on where your items come from. Some crystal-mining and plant-harvesting practices are destructive to the Earth and also exploit workers and communities. Search for ethical companies to support and if you can't find an ethical option you can always go without or get creative with what you already have. It's not always easy to get this right or be perfect with this, but you will find that tools sourced with good and conscious intentions will support you in wonderful ways.

PREPARING A MAGICAL SPACE

Before you begin to work with magical tools, it's a good idea to have a dedicated magical space to work in. Having a space where you can both keep your tools and perform your manifestation rituals can add a lot of power to your practices. This space can be anywhere that works for you and your lifestyle; it can be a beautiful altar, a cushion in a corner of a room, the edge of your bed or even a spot at the kitchen table.

The more prayers, spells, intentions, devotion and manifestation you do in a place, the more amplified the energy becomes each time. Every time you show up to this space, you're adding a new layer, and on those days when you feel tired or uninspired all you need to do is just show up to your sacred space and be.

MAKE YOUR OWN AURA SPRAY

Aura sprays can be used in many ways, from spritzing and cleansing your aura and your sacred space to cleansing and cleaning magical items and surfaces. Get creative with essential oils and come up with your own blends (see page 131 for oil ideas).

You will need:

- *Incense, sage or palo santo*
- *A clean bottle (coloured glass is ideal, but as always, use what you have) with a spray lid attachment*
- *Salt*
- *Crystal chips, dried herbs, dried flowers (optional)*
- *5 drops of sage or white sage essential oil*
- *2 drops of Frankincense essential oil*
- *Vodka (25ml for each 100ml bottle)*
- *Water – distilled, bottled or filtered works best*

1. *Get all your materials together. Burn some incense, sage or palo santo smoke inside the bottle to clear it.*
2. *Drop a pinch of salt into the bottle and add in any flowers, herbs or crystals you are using.*
3. *Add 5 drops of sage or white sage oil and 2 drops of Frankincense. Put your nose to the bottle and see how the blend smells to you and then alter it to your liking.*
4. *Add the vodka to the bottle, then fill the rest of the bottle with water.*
5. *Charge the bottle on your altar, under a full moon, or in your own hands.*

HOW TO CREATE AN ALTAR

An altar is a sacred space that acts as portal between you and the divine. You can sit at your altar for meditation, prayer and manifestation practices, or whenever you just want to connect with your own heart and return to yourself.

You will need:

- *Duster or cloth*
- *Sage, palo santo or incense or an aura spray*
- *Altar cloth, a scarf or bandana*
- *Sacred objects:*
- *something to represent the four elements – a candle for fire (be careful with candles if using a middle section of a shelf as this can be a fire hazard), incense for air, crystals, flowers or plants for earth and a bowl of water or shells for water*
- *images or statues of angels, saints or other deities you have a connection with*
- *photos of your ancestors*
- *items that have special meaning for you (gifts, heirlooms, things you've had since you were young, and so on)*
- *spiritual quotes*
- *your favourite spiritual books*

1. *Find a space that works for you where you won't be disturbed by others – a small table, a shelf, the top of a bookcase, your bedside table, even a corner of your desk will do. Make sure this is a space that will be easy for you to visit and even just walk past often.*
2. *Physically clear the space – remove any objects you don't want in the space, then dust and wipe down your surface.*
3. *Energetically clear the space. Using sage, palo santo or incense, waft the smoke above, beneath and around the space. You can also use an aura spray for this or just visualise white light clearing the space.*
4. *Lay a cloth down if you have one. Make sure it's clean and ironed. You can use a specifically designed altar cloth, or a scarf or bandana can work well too.*
5. *Begin to place sacred objects in the space with intention, then activate your altar. Take a moment to light a candle, visualise the*

space filled with gold light and say: This altar is now activated. May this space be clear and protected and may it work as a portal to connect me to my guides, angels and inner light. And so it is, and so it is, and so it is.

STATIONERY SUPPLIES

You've already been working with a journal and it's a great idea to keep using it as you work with your manifesting practices and rituals. Journals are good for noting down how you're feeling, what you're thinking and any insights, cosmic downloads or epiphanies you have along the road.

A grimoire is a book that you use especially for magical work. In this book you can write down your dreams, spells and rituals, what's working or not working in your manifestation practices, the deities you're calling on and anything else that feels important to note down as you work and weave your magic. It's also always a good idea to have loose paper handy for burning rituals, spells, writing affirmations or writing down other quick notes.

You can use any kind of pens or pencils in your practices, but if you are planning on burning what you've written consider writing in pencil as burning felt tip is not always so pleasant.

CRYSTALS

Many of the rituals in this book will include suggestions for crystals to use, but you can make any substitutions from this list or use a clear quartz as a replacement for anything. If you don't have any crystals you can use pebbles or stones that you find out in nature, pieces of shaped or smooth glass (nothing that can cut you, please!) or even something made out of metal like a pendant or even a paperclip can be used as a conductor of energy.

Working with crystals is a deeply personal and intuitive thing. You may find you're drawn to a crystal for use in your manifesting that isn't traditionally used for that purpose. Always trust your intuition when working with crystals and go with what feels right for you.

The following is by no means a definitive list, but it should get you started if you're new to working with crystals.

ALL-PURPOSE MANIFESTATION CRYSTALS

- *Clear quartz*
- *Golden/Imperial topaz*
- *Rutilated quartz*
- *Lemurian quartz*
- *Kundalini quartz*
- *Merlinite*

CRYSTALS FOR LOVE AND RELATIONSHIPS

- *Rose quartz (all-purpose love and relationships)*
- *Rhodonite (self-love)*
- *Pink kunzite (unconditional love)*
- *Emerald (successful relationships)*
- *Malachite (heart healing)*
- *Pink tourmaline (compassion)*
- *Pink opal (heart opening)*
- *Ruby (sexuality)*

CRYSTALS FOR PROSPERITY AND ABUNDANCE

- *Citrine (abundance)*
- *Pyrite (law of attraction)*
- *Green jade (fortune)*
- *Green aventurine (luck)*
- *Topaz (generosity)*
- *Moss agate (new beginnings)*
- *Chrysoprase (money attractor)*
- *Amber (wealth)*

CRYSTALS FOR WORK AND SUCCESS

- *Amazonite (life purpose)*
- *Pyrite (success and prosperity)*
- *Ametrine (intuition, success)*
- *Tiger's eye (power)*
- *Sunstone (energy, action)*
- *Peridot (transformation, self-belief)*
- *Fluorite (learning and wisdom)*
- *Sodalite (writing and communication)*
- *Carnelian (confidence)*

CRYSTALS FOR HARMONY AND HOME

- *Blue calcite (harmony)*
- *Smokey quartz (grounding, protection)*
- *Hematite (boundaries)*
- *Howlite (calming)*
- *Lepidolite (worry-free)*

- *Selenite (clarity, cleansing)*
- *Turquoise (meditation, peace)*
- *Dalmatian jasper (joy, happiness)*

CRYSTALS FOR SPIRITUAL GROWTH

- *Amethyst (intuition)*
- *Labradorite (transformation, third eye)*
- *Moonstone (psychic awareness)*
- *Blue kyanite (truth)*
- *Herkimer diamond (high vibrations)*
- *Black obsidian (grounding, protection)*
- *Celestite or Angelite (angelic realms)*
- *Lemurian quartz (awakening)*

OILS

As with the crystals included in this book, the list of oils is just a guideline, a starting-off point. You can always use what you have or what you feel intuitively drawn to using.

ALL-PURPOSE MANIFESTATION OILS

- *Vetiver*
- *Lemon*
- *Jasmine*

OILS FOR LOVE AND RELATIONSHIPS

- *Rose*
- *Ylang-ylang*
- *Bergamot*

OILS FOR PROSPERITY AND ABUNDANCE

- *Orange*
- *Cinnamon*
- *Chamomile*

OILS FOR WORK AND SUCCESS

- *Basil*
- *Irish moss*
- *Cypress*

OILS FOR HARMONY AND HOME

- *Sage*
- *Rosemary*
- *Lavender*

OILS FOR SPIRITUAL GROWTH

- *Frankincense*
- *Sandalwood*
- *Spikenard*

HERBS

Again, the following list is just to get you started. Use your intuition and what's available to you in your garden and kitchen cupboard! Although not technically a herb or a spice, having some salt on hand is always useful too.

ALL-PURPOSE MANIFESTATION HERBS AND SPICES

- *Bay leaf*
- *Cinnamon*
- *Thyme*

HERBS AND SPICES FOR LOVE AND RELATIONSHIPS

- *Vanilla*
- *Mint*
- *Chilli (to spice things up!)*

HERBS FOR PROSPERITY AND ABUNDANCE

- *Oregano*
- *Saffron*
- *Marjoram*

HERBS AND SPICES FOR WORK AND SUCCESS

- *Allspice*
- *Pepper*
- *Cloves*

HERBS FOR HARMONY AND HOME

- *Sage*
- *Chamomile*
- *Lavender*

HERBS FOR SPIRITUAL GROWTH

- *Angelica*
- *Rosemary*
- *Cacao*

INCENSE

The burning of incense or herb bundles can be useful in your manifestation practices, especially in setting up your spaces and clearing negativity before you begin. You can use any incense you have or are drawn to, or bundles of dried herbs – including sage and rosemary, or cypress, eucalyptus, or flowers. Palo santo is also a good option.

TAROT AND ORACLE CARDS

Using a tarot or oracle deck alongside your manifestation practices can help you to dive deeper into your own psyche and receive messages from your guides. They can also be used to enhance spells, be placed on your altar or as a reminder of what you are working towards. You can use any deck you have, print one from online or make your own.

CAULDRONS

A small cast-iron cauldron can be useful in manifestation for burning incense and burning papers. They can also be used for holding your dreams and wishes (see the section on working with a goddess box on page 152).

CRAFT SUPPLIES

A collection of craft supplies will be useful for vision boarding, art journalling, decorating your altar, and so on. Some things you may like to have on hand are craft paper, scissors, glue, magazines, coloured pens and pencils, markers, glitter and whatever else your inner child desires.

SIMPLE PRACTICES FOR MANIFESTATION

The following are all-purpose manifestation practices that can be used to manifest anything you need or want. Make these practices your own, make them work for you and your life, and most of all have fun!

SAY IT OUT LOUD

It's simple, but it works. Right now, just go ahead and say out loud what it is you want to manifest. You don't have to say it to anyone, just say it. Say: *I want [whatever you want] to manifest in my life.* Let those words ring out and vibrate through the universe.

Whisper what you want to yourself as you lie in bed at night, while looking in the mirror, while making a cup of tea. Just say the words. It doesn't have to be anything fancy; you may just say: *I'd really like [this thing]!*, or: *Wouldn't it be nice to have [this thing]?*, or even: *[This thing] is manifesting for me now!*

There are two schools of thought when it comes to telling other people about your dreams. One says to never tell anyone about them, so as to keep them safe, but another idea is to tell everyone and anyone you meet about your dreams and goals. You never know who can help you, or who may know someone who can help your dream to come true.

Some dreams may need to be kept safe, others may need to be shouted from the rafters. Always do what feels right for you, but speak your dreams out loud even if it's just to yourself and your guides.

WRITE IT DOWN

When you write down what you want, you're taking that thought, that idea, that desire into the physical. You are recording it. You're etching it. You're intending it.

Take a piece of paper and write down something you are working on manifesting in the present tense, such as: *[What you want] is now manifesting for me.* Underneath it, write *And so it is* three times.

Now turn the paper one-quarter clockwise (this brings the energy towards you) and write *And so it is* all across the paper on this new angle. As you do this, really connect with your desire for this to happen. Feel it happening, believe it's happening. Turn the paper another quarter and do the same, then turn it again and repeat the process.

You'll end up with a piece of paper that looks like a bunch of scribbles, but each *And so it is* is a cementing of your intention, a will for it to happen, a little piece of magic. Play around with different phrases to write over the top of your manifestations. Try *this manifests now*, or *manifest, manifest, manifest!* Use any phrase or words that resonate with you, just do it with intention. If you like, instead of writing over your words you can just write *and so it is* at the bottom or write in a circle, making a frame of *and so it is, and so it is*, around what you have written.

Plant your paper in the earth, burn it in a fire ceremony, keep it under your pillow or in your goddess box, in a favourite book or somewhere safe. You may just come across it later when it's manifested for you!

VISUALISATION

One of the most well-known, tried, tested and true manifestation practices is visualisation. There's been a lot of research done on the power of visualisation and many high-level athletes and people who've reached the top of their field swear by its power.

Visualisation helps you to re-wire your brain and shifts your vibration to a point where you just expect your dreams to come true. When you expect good things to happen you're more likely to make them happen – and also to notice them when they do!

Visualisation practice

Whenever you need or want something, visualise it happening in the way you want it to. Visualise the meeting going well, visualise the local shop having the ingredients you need for a recipe or spell, visualise things turning out as you would like them to. When you do this, really try to feel it's happening. Visualise how you're feeling, the space you're in, the temperature of the room, the smells, the sounds, what you're wearing, the sensations on your skin. Really let yourself practise experiencing the outcome that you desire. Make it real within you so it becomes real in the physical.

Your perfect day

This is a fantastic visualisation exercise to practise as often as you like.

Prepare yourself for meditation. Take a few deep breaths into your heart space and relax. Visualise yourself filled with white light and surrounded by blue light. See your third eye opening and activating. Now take yourself through a visualisation journey of your perfect day. See yourself waking up. Where are you? What does the bed feel like? What does the room look like? Visualise yourself going through your day, getting out of bed, making breakfast, getting ready for your day. Where are you going today? What will you be doing? Go through your whole day in this way until it's time to get back into bed again.

You can take as long as you like doing this practice and you can change it as often as you like. You can also try visualising your perfect day tomorrow, in a few weeks' or months' time, or even in a few years.

Your perfect day will change and evolve, so don't worry about getting every detail just right; this is a practice for creating the life you most want to live.

GRAB YOUR JOURNAL!

Write down your perfect day in present tense, for example: *I'm waking up in the most comfortable bed in my brand-new house while sunlight streams through the windows …* You can be as specific as you like or keep things vague if you're not sure exactly what you want things to look like just yet. If you struggle with the description of what's happening, focus on the feelings: *I wake up feeling refreshed and excited about my day …*

MANIFESTATION ALTARS

Working with a manifestation altar is like creating a miniature, physical version of what you want to see manifest in your life. Everything on your manifestation altar should be aligned with the intention of what you want to manifest. Don't focus too much on making your altar look pretty, working altars rarely look Instagram-worthy. It's more important that this altar represents what you want to call into your life. Focus on the intention over the aesthetic and it will end up looking beautiful anyway!

Your manifestation altar can be very specific (such as calling in a new best friend) or it can be more general (such as being open to love in all forms).

Some items that work well on manifestation altars are:

- *Crystals, plants or flowers that align with your intention.*
- *Spell candles dressed with oils specific to your manifestation.*
- *Images, art, prayer cards or oracle cards featuring deities who can help with this particular manifestation.*
- *Oracle or tarot cards featuring images and symbols of what you are calling in.*
- *Objects relating to what you want to manifest (such as a paper clip for work, an airline ticket for travel, best friends charms for friendships, and so on).*
- *Books about what you want to manifest – such as money, success, love, and so on.*

To create your manifestation altar, first prepare, clear and cleanse your space (see page 149 for how to do this) – a good place is somewhere you'll see it often, such as your desk, a shelf in your main living area or your bedside table. Then place your items on your altar with intention.

Activate your altar by lighting a candle and saying: *This altar is now activated. May this space be clear and protected and may it work as a portal for my manifestation. As this altar activates I now call in [what you are manifesting] and so it is, and so it is, and so it is.* Take a moment to visualise your altar shining bright and becoming a magnet to what you want to call in.

Check in with your altar every day. Take a look at what you've placed there, light the candle again, and if it burns down, replace it with a new one. Replace any flowers that begin to wilt and generally keep your altar looking clean, clear and fresh. Meditate at your altar, say prayers, talk to your guides, whatever helps you feel connected to what you are manifesting.

When your desire has manifested or when you just intuitively feel like it's time to clear your altar and make a new one (for the same purpose or something new), give thanks and then tidy up your altar, putting everything away and starting over.

VISION BOARDS

Creating a vision board is one of the most popular, fun, easy and powerful ways to get what you want. Similar to working with altars, this is another way to create a physical representation of what it is that you want to see made manifest in your life. Vision boards help you to stay focused on your goals, constantly reminding you of what you want and what you're creating. The process of creating a vision board is deeply intuitive and can even help you to figure out what it is you want in the process.

HOW TO CREATE A CRAFT VISION BOARD

You can make a vision board for a particular area of your life, such as success at work or in love, or you can make a general vision board that covers things you want to manifest in all areas of your life.

You will need:

- *Craft materials*
- *Candle and incense*
- *Oracle card*
- *Journal*
- *Magazines*
- *Scissors*
- *Vision board*
- *Glue*

1. *Prepare your space and gather your craft materials. If you like you could light a candle and some incense and play some high-vibrational music or mantras.*
2. *Get yourself into a relaxed, centred and intuitive state. Take a few moments to close your eyes, take a few deep breaths – whatever helps you to centre yourself. You may also like to call in your guides to help you.*
3. *Set an intention for what it is you want this vision board to help you manifest. You can do this by placing an oracle card on the table in*

front of you, writing a few words down in your journal or saying it out loud. If you are creating an all-purpose vision board, just let that be your intention.

4. *Begin by going through your magazines and looking for images, words or anything else that aligns with your intention. Let this be an intuitive process and try to get into a creative flow. Cut out anything you're drawn to, even if it's not in alignment with your original intention. Your images and words don't have to be literal expressions of what you want, they can be symbolic or just represent a feeling. Get creative! This is all about your own communication system with the divine and your own higher self, so use pictures and words that make sense to you even if no one else would understand them.*

5. *Once you have your pile of images and words ready, take some time to go through them and decide which ones you want to add to your vision board. During this part of the process your intention may evolve and your vision board may go in a different direction than what you were planning. Just go with it and follow your intuition.*

6. *Without gluing anything down yet, place your images and words and anything else you've found on your board backing. Move things around until it looks the way you want it.*

7. *As you begin to glue everything onto your board imagine that the glue is creating a solid setting of your intention; it's the sowing of the seed. The glue is the prayer, the communication with the divine and your higher self and you're telling them – this is what you really want. Take your gluing seriously; this is powerful magic!*

8. *Once everything is glued down you may like to add some eco-glitter to the edges or throw a handful over your vision board as a way to 'activate' the magic.*

9. *Step back and look at what you've created, then let it manifest!*

10. *Put your vision board somewhere you'll see it every day. Over your desk or by your bed is ideal, but if you have to, you can always put it inside a cupboard door or somewhere only you can see it. You can even take a photo of your vision board and make it your lock screen on your phone or laptop. Every time you look at your vision board trust that everything you've asked for is manifesting in your life.*

HOW TO CREATE A DIGITAL VISION BOARD

If you don't have access to craft materials or just don't vibe with the idea of crafting, you can also make a digital vision board. The system for this is the same as above but instead of looking through magazines you can look through Pinterest or other free-image sites online. Then instead of sticking your images onto card, make your vision board on Pinterest or create a collage in Photoshop, Paint or an app like Canva. Print out your collage and put it up somewhere you'll see it often or make it your phone lock screen so you'll see it every time you pick up your phone.

MAKE A WISH LIST

Ideally, this should be done digitally, so you can change it easily. Excel, Word or a notes app is perfect for this, or you can go analogue and use good old paper and pen if you like. Basically, this is the creation of a wish list of everything you want to manifest. You can have different sections for different things or just create one big list.

List everything you want to manifest – material items, how you want to feel, opportunities, the types of relationships you want … Whatever you want, list it. Don't go overboard here; try to keep the list under twenty things so you don't get manifesting overwhelm. Put these items in order, with what you most want at the top.

Return to this list as often as you like but at least once a month. Doing this at the New or Full Moon is powerful. Go through your list often and notice what's manifested and what you may no longer want. Move things around depending on importance. Add things that you now want to manifest.

Keeping a track of your dreams like this can help you to stay focused on where you're headed and make sure you're still going in the direction of your dreams.

RITUAL BATHS

Ritual bathing can be used as a way to soak up the energies of what you're wanting to manifest. Think of a ritual bath as a way to infuse your intention into your physical body and your aura, which, as mentioned earlier, can act as a magnet for what you want. There are many ways to do a ritual bath, and as with most of these practices it's always most powerful when you tap into your own creativity and intuition. The following is just one example of how to work with ritual baths.

Although this example includes magical items, you can have a simple ritual bath with just water and soap if that's all you have. Just hold the soap or bubble bath in your hands and activate it with your intention before you begin, or just put your intention into the water!

1. *Set an intention for what you'd like to soak in, then gather supplies that align with your intention – salts, herbs, flowers, crystals and oils. (See page 131 for more information on oils and herbs and page 129*

for more information on crystals.) *Always check if the oils you are using are safe to put on your skin and if the crystals are safe to soak in water.

2. *Take a moment to centre and ground your energy with some deep breaths and visualise yourself clear and grounded.*

3. *As you run the water, stay connected to your intention. When the bath is full, begin to add your ingredients. Each time you place an item in the bath say out loud what it is for. For example:* Salt for cleansing any negativity or anything that's not in alignment with my desire, roses for romance. *Continue to place in your herbs, crystals, oils and flowers, and as you do so, continue to state your intention for each item.*

4. *As you lower yourself into the bath, visualise yourself moving into and merging with the energy of what you're manifesting.*

5. *As you sit in the bath and let yourself soak, enjoy the feeling of fully absorbing your intention. While you're in the bath you can speak with your guides, the divine or your higher self. Chant mantras, visualise or just meditate on what you want.*

6. *When you're ready, give thanks to the water and all the plant and crystal allies you've worked with. As you step out of the bath, see yourself stepping into the next chapter, radiant and ready to make your dreams come true.*

7. *Dispose of any remaining plant items by giving them back to the earth or putting them in with your plant waste. Wash your crystals for re-use.*

CRYSTALS

Programming crystals for manifestation is a fun and easy way to turn a crystal into a magnet for your desires. You can do this with any crystals that you wear or with a small one that you can carry in your pocket or your bra.

You will need:

- *Crystal or clear quartz*
- *Water, salt water, incense or sage smoke or white light, to cleanse*

1. *To programme a crystal for manifestation, choose a crystal that aligns with what you want to manifest, or just use a piece of clear quartz.*
2. *Start by cleansing your crystal. You can do this with water, salt water, incense or sage smoke, your breath or white light. Check that the crystal you are using is not water-soluble before submerging.*
3. *Hold the crystal in your right hand at your heart centre and take a few deep breaths. Whisper into the crystal what it is you'd like it to help you manifest. For example,* I activate this crystal with the energy of love. As I carry this crystal, I draw to me the most perfect, loving romantic partner that is in alignment with my best and highest good. *You can say a few simple words or have a long chat with your crystal telling it in detail what you'd like it to help you with.*
4. *Hold the crystal at your third eye and visualise what it is that you want.*
5. *Hold the crystal at your heart again and take a few more deep breaths.*
6. *Thank your crystal for supporting your manifesting.*

7. *Carry your crystal with you like a talisman and know that it's lit up and activated and helping attract to you what you most desire.*

8. *Clear and repeat as often as you intuitively feel you need to.*

TAROT AND ORACLE CARDS

There are a number of ways you can use tarot and oracle cards in your manifesting.

- *Choose cards that visually represent what you'd like to manifest and place them where you will see them often – on your altar, your desk, your fridge, and so on.*
- *Take a photo of a card that aligns with your manifestation and make it the lock screen on your phone.*
- *Carry a card depicting what you want to manifest with you in your purse, pocket or car. (This may make your cards a little dog-eared, so you might want to use a deck you don't use for readings, or buy a second copy of a deck you love.)*
- *Put cards showing what you want to manifest on display or on your altar while working with any manifestation rituals and practices.*
- *Choose cards that align with your dreams and journal on them. Write about how they make you feel and anything else that comes up for you.*
- *Glue cards onto your vision board (again, you might want to use a second or spare deck for this!).*
- *Do a reading for yourself but choose the cards face up that you want to see in your potential outcome position.*
- *Do a simple candle spell by choosing a card that represents your desire and lighting a candle in front of it.*

CANDLE SPELLS

One of the simplest and most effective spells is a candle spell. You only need a few items, and this can be used for just about anything you want to manifest.

You will need:

- *Incense, sage smoke or aura spray*
- *A white candle (small wish candles work well)*
- *A candle holder or a heatproof plate*
- *Something sharp to etch into the candle – a crystal point, earring back or drawing pin*
- *Oils and herbs of your choosing (optional)*

1. *Cleanse and prepare your space for your candle spell. Ideally, place your candle spell on your altar, or use any flat, safe surface you have available. Just make sure it's clean and tidy and energetically clear.*
2. *Use incense, sage smoke or aura spray to clear yourself and the space.*
3. *Prepare your energy by taking a few deep breaths and visualising yourself clear, grounded and protected. See yourself and your space surrounded by a bright blue light.*
4. *Hold the candle at your heart and visualise what you want to manifest.*
5. *Etch into the candle any words, phrases or symbols that represent what you're calling in.*
6. *Dress your candle with the oil of your choosing, rubbing the oil into the candle from top to bottom to symbolise drawing the energy down towards you.*
7. *Pat on any herbs you've chosen to work with or roll your candle in them.*

8. *Say out loud or visualise what it is you want to manifest. Call on your guides, angels, ancestors, higher self, whoever you would like to support you. Take as long as you like communing with the divine and visualising your desire manifesting.*

9. *When you feel you're holding the vision in your heart, light the candle.*

10. *Thank your guides, angels and anyone else you called in to help you.*

11. *Let the candle burn all the way to the bottom. If you need to pause the candle, use a snuffer to put it out, then relight it when you can.*

12. *When the candle has burned down, give your thanks and trust that what you have asked for is on its way to you.*

13. *Dispose of the wax remains by putting them in the bin, or you can keep them on your altar until your spell manifests.*

SYMBOLS AND SIGILS

Creating and using symbols or sigils is another form of weaving your intention into the physical. You can use any symbol that already exists or create a sigil, which is your personal symbol created with the intention you want it to hold. Creating sigils can be done in numerous ways. You can draw something intuitively or see the section on manifesting Work and Purpose (page 175) for another powerful way to create your own sigils.

SOME SYMBOLS THAT WORK WELL IN MANIFESTING ARE:

- *Pound or dollar signs for money and work.*
- *Hearts for romance and relationships.*

- *Stars for high vibrations or connection to your higher self.*
- *Suns for positivity and joy.*
- *Eyes for protection.*
- *Pentagram for power and protection.*
- *Fire element symbol for energy and movement.*
- *Earth element symbol for grounding your manifestation.*
- *Squares for stability.*
- *Triangles for spiritual connection.*

Once you have chosen a symbol or sigil you can use it amplify your manifesting. Draw it anywhere and everywhere you feel called. You can draw your symbols or sigils with pen or pencil or just using your finger. Draw them on candles as part of your spellwork, on pieces of paper you carry in your pocket, on rental applications, online dating profiles, credit cards or cash, your phone, laptop, wrists, third eye, glasses of water, on anything you want to activate with your intention and magic.

PRAYER

You don't need to follow a religion to draw on the power of prayer. Prayer is essentially just a conversation with the divine, whatever form that takes for you.

Take some time to just speak to the divine in your own words, tell the universe how you're feeling, what you need help with and what you want to manifest in your life. Let this be a friendly, casual conversation. Just talk – at your altar, while looking up at the night sky, in the car, in the shower, anywhere you like. Open up a dialogue. Keep letting the universe know where you're at and what you need. Have a chat, get to know each other. Oh, and don't forget to listen. You may just start hearing the answers to your questions and guidance on how to make your dreams come true!

GODDESS BOX

A goddess box (sometimes referred to as a god box) is like a letter box to the divine. Write down whatever it is that you want to manifest, then put it in your god box. Visualise this like putting in your requests to the universe. As you place your notes in the box, see them lighting up and your requests being received.

This is fantastic practice in asking for what you want. No matter how big or small your desire, write it down and put it in the box. It's always a nice idea to give thanks for the things that have manifested in your life, so you may like to occasionally put a note in saying thank you for everything you've received so far.

Once your goddess box is full you may like to go back and read over what you've asked for and notice just how many things have manifested. If you come across things that haven't come to pass and you still want them, place them back in. Everything that has manifested can either be burned or recycled with love and gratitude.

MANTRAS

Working with mantras is an ancient and very effective way to manifest. Mantras can change the patterns of the mind, helping you to release, clear and shift blocks and limiting thoughts. They can also help elevate your energy and the energy of your space. You can use mantras in any language from Hindi to Gurmukhi to Sanskrit. You can even recite mantras in English. As you chant along or just listen to mantras you are raising your vibration, shifting into a higher energetic state and aligning to your highest dreams and destiny.

Do some research by searching for mantras for the specific things you want to manifest. Try searching for manifestation mantras or money mantras. Make a playlist of your favourite mantras and listen to it often. You don't have to chant mantras for them to be effective, you can just listen to them while you go about your day, on your commute, while you work or make dinner. If want to sing along, don't worry about getting the pronunciation correct, just do your best, it's all about the intention and heart you put into the practice.

Listening to mantras while you do your other manifestation practices is a powerful way to amp up the energy.

CAUSAL CHAKRA ACTIVATION

The causal chakra is a transcendental (meaning outside the physical body) chakra and sits just above and behind your crown. This chakra is your own personal moon that connects you to your guides and angels, but it can also be activated so that it becomes a beacon of light, calling to you the people, situations and outcomes that are in alignment with your best and highest good.

HOW TO ACTIVATE THE CAUSAL CHAKRA

1. *Begin by getting comfortable, relaxed, centred and grounded.*
2. *Take a few deep breaths and begin to see your heart opening and expanding.*

3. *See yourself filled with gold light and surrounded by a protective blue light.*

4. *Send your awareness up to your causal chakra above and behind the crown. See this chakra glowing a beautiful bright silver.*

5. *Focus on what you want to manifest and see this light expanding, pulsing and reaching far and wide, calling this to you.*

6. *Ask that all that is in alignment with your best and highest good will find you. Ask that your highest destiny will find you. Ask that all the people, places, situations and opportunities that are in perfect alignment with your dreams will find you.*

7. *See this light radiating out in all directions, activating and reaching all those who can help you manifest your dreams. See this light becoming a magnet for everything that will help you live your best possible life.*

8. *When you feel ready, let that light come back into your causal chakra. See that chakra still glowing bright, still drawing to you everything you need and want.*

9. *Take a few deep breaths and come back into your body.*

10. *Visualise your causal chakra shining bright whenever you want to activate, call in and draw in your desires.*

MAGICAL GOAL SETTING

It may not seem that magical but setting goals can help get you where you want to go in a focused, aligned and often very fast way.

Here are some magical ways to set goals:

- *Align your goals with the Earth's cycles and set long-term goals at the equinoxes and solstices.*

- *Set goals by the moon. Set bigger goals for longer moon cycles, such as the six-month cycle from the New Moon to the Full Moon in the same sign. Set smaller goals by the shorter cycles, such as from the New to the Full Moon, or the New Moon to the next New Moon.*
- *Keep a note of your goals somewhere magical. Write them on paper or card and put them on your altar, use a special magical goal-setting book, make a magical Excel spreadsheet.*
- *Revisit your goals often. Change them, add to them, remove ones that no longer resonate. Your goals should evolve with you.*
- *Work towards your goals. Creating goals is powerful intention-setting work, but they only work when you do. Show up, do your part and make them happen!*

MANIFESTING WITH EMOTION

Strong emotional states can add a huge amount of energy and power to your manifesting. How you're feeling when you ask for what you want can be just as important, or more so, as the words you use. Sometimes the most incredible things can manifest simply from you being in a heightened emotional state and calling out for the universe to help you, or just setting a very strong intention in an emotional moment.

Next time you're experiencing a big feeling, go ahead and ask for what you need or want. Close your eyes, take a breath, and ask for it. This can work well when you're frustrated at a situation that doesn't feel in alignment for you any more, but try to avoid doing this when feeling anger, rage, resentment or any other feelings that may cause you to send out energetic fireballs to others.

Manifesting with emotion works especially well when you're feeling good, grateful, joyful or just sensing those high vibrations.

GIVING AND RECEIVING

Manifesting often focuses on receiving, but it's easier to receive when the energy flows both ways. To be able to receive, you have to be able to give.

If you are in a position to give to charity (even just a few quid when you can), give your time to a cause you feel strongly about, or help a friend in need, you may find it not only gives you the warm fuzzies knowing you're making a difference and helping someone else, but also helps unlock and unblock your manifesting.

Giving doesn't have to be big or costly, it can be as simple as giving compliments, making dinner for someone you love, donating clothing or blankets or popping your spare change in a tip jar. Don't underestimate the power of small acts of generosity.

CONNECT WITH MAGICAL PEOPLE

Surrounding yourself with other people who are working on themselves and working on making their dreams come true can have a huge impact on your ability to manifest. Being able to share your dreams with people who will support you and celebrate your success is so important on this journey.

You don't need to cut everyone who's less supportive out of your life for good, but the more you surround yourself with people who do support you and also even dream big themselves, the easier it will be to make things happen. We aren't meant to do this alone! Be discerning about who you trust with your dreams and whose advice you take, and if you don't have a lot of people supporting your dreams it may be time to call some new people into your life.

Here are some ways to find your people:

- *Go to manifesting events, spiritual workshops or moon meet-ups online or in person.*
- *Hang out at yoga studios, gyms or any other places where people are setting goals and showing up for them.*
- *Find a group to meditate with; people who meditate are usually on a path to higher awareness.*
- *Join online groups and make an effort to post and comment; ask if anyone wants to connect one-on-one or in person.*
- *Talk to people who are already in your life about your goals and dreams and ask them about theirs. You may already have more supporters than you realise!*

TAKING ACTION

The most powerful manifestation practice of all is taking action. There are times when things just happen, when magical opportunities just appear, when things seem to fall into your lap. But most of the time, even then, there's been some action taken on your part. Whether you're showing up for the inner work, meditating and chanting mantras or applying for jobs and going on blind dates, taking action is where your power truly lies.

So many of these practices simply help activate and expand your inner power so you can show up and make your life happen. Believe in yourself, hold a vision for an amazing future, believe it can and will happen for you, but you also have to take those steps forward, those leaps of faith, and put yourself out there if you really want to live your dream life.

Don't just visualise the dream job, apply for it. Don't just bathe in prosperity, take control of your finances. Don't just carry around your activated rose quartz, put yourself out there and start meeting people.

Show up for your dreams and they will show up in your life.

MANIFESTATION RITUALS

This section includes detailed rituals you can work with to manifest your dreams in each of the areas of:

- *Love and relationships*
- *Money and abundance*
- *Work and purpose*
- *Home and harmony*

Each of these rituals is broken down into:

- *Affirmations – use these (or create your own!) any way you like alongside your manifesting rituals.*
- *Cleansing ritual – this will help you make space for what you want to bring in.*
- *Mindset ritual – here you'll be guided in how to remove any mindset blocks and get clear on your intention.*
- *Energy ritual – this ritual will help you shift your energy and vibration into alignment with what you want to manifest.*
- *Magic ritual – your chance to get a little witchy and ground your intention into the physical world.*
- *Practical magic – how to get out there and make it happen!*

These rituals can be followed exactly as they are, or you can make them your own, using what resonates and leaving the rest. It's a good idea, though, to avoid jumping straight to the Magic Ritual. The preparation rituals are provided so that you can go into this process with your mind, heart and soul awakened so you can consciously manifest your dreams in alignment with your best and highest good.

You can set aside an afternoon to work with a ritual in full or take your time working with the preparation rituals in your own time before performing the Magic Ritual.

MANIFESTING LOVE AND RELATIONSHIPS RITUAL

The following ritual can be used to bring more of any kind of love into your life – romantic love, self-love, friendship, family love, new connections and relationships, or just a deeper feeling of love for the divine, the universe and your life. You can use this ritual to make your current relationships better as well as call in new ones.

Remember that you can use the tools listed here, any of the alternatives listed in the Magical Supplies section, use what you already have, or go without. It's all about intention. Also remember that you can't make a specific person fall in love with you or become your new best friend. Call for the right people to come in and you may meet someone even better.

AFFIRMATIONS:

My heart shines so bright and clear that nothing and no one can
   harm me.
My heart is open to all that is love.
I am love, I attract love and I receive love.
I am a magnet for healthy loving relationships.

THE CLEANSING RITUAL

To make space for new and deeper love and more aligned relationships
to enter your life it's helpful to first clear away the energetic connections
you still have with those who are no longer in your life.

If you want to call in new love, release the hold that any ex-loves have
on you. If you want to call in new, supportive friendships release any
negativity and hurt from old friendships. And if you want to grow your
family or bring new positive dynamics into your family relationships it's
helpful to release and heal what's come before.

Even when people are no longer present in your physical life you may
still have energetic cords that keep you connected to people from your past.

You may still have a connection or energetic cord with someone if:

- *Years later you still find yourself thinking about them or a specific
  situation they were involved in.*
- *You have dreams about them.*
- *You're still holding on to some anger or pain that they caused you.*
- *You still can't forgive what they did.*
- *You can't forgive yourself for something you did to them.*
- *You compare your new relationships to them.*

Energetic cords are created in all relationships. Some cords are filled with love and support and lift you up, some cords drain your energy and keep you stuck from moving forward. When a relationship ends (even amicably), when one person does all the giving and doesn't receive anything in return, or when a relationship is based on control and manipulation, cords of energy can become trapped.

Energy cords can develop from any part of your auric field and energy body, but they often attach to the solar plexus, the shoulders, the back or root chakra at the base of the spine. Clearing these cords is a very simple process and can take just a few minutes. You may find that you need to repeat this process a few times before you start to feel like the connection is cleared, but the simple intention of wanting to be released is often enough to get it shifting.

You can clear negative cords of attachment whether the person is still in your life or not, and even if they have passed over. All you are really doing here is releasing the negative attachment and setting yourself free of the hold they have on you, or even any hold you have on them too.

Note – if you've experienced a particularly difficult relationship you may need to work with a professional alongside your energy work.

VISUALISATION

1. *Centre your energy with a few deep breaths. See yourself filled with white light and surrounded by blue light.*
2. *Bring to mind the person you'd like to energetically release.*
3. *Visualise the energy cord between you. You may see or get a sense of where the cord is attached on your body or even how big or small it*

*is, what colour it is, and so on. If you don't see or feel anything,
simply visualise a clear cord between you (like plastic tubing).*

4. *If you can, send a beam of love down the cord and wish them well.
   See this as a bright pink light from your heart to theirs.*
5. *Now see the cord cutting, dissolving and dropping away from your
   body and from theirs. See the cord shrivelling up and disappearing
   into light.*
6. *Affirm out loud or in your head:* I love you and I let you go. *Or just:*
   I let you go.
7. *See yourself clear and aligned and free. You are now only connected
   to this person through memory, love and grace. They no longer have
   any energetic hold on you.*

If you feel that the visualisation alone is not enough, you can take a piece
of paper and draw two stick figures. Write your name and their name on
the top of each stick figure. Draw a cord between you. Write along the
cord what you feel is keeping you connected – for example, fear of not
finding anyone else, shared history, and so on. Take a deep breath and the
piece of paper and either cut or tear the paper through the cord
symbolising the cutting of the cord between you.

Shred or recycle the paper.

THE MINDSET RITUAL

Take some time to think about, meditate on and journal about what kind
of love you want to manifest into your life.

GRAB YOUR JOURNAL!

Answer the following questions in your journal:

- *Why do you want to manifest more love into your life?*
- *How will having more love in your life benefit you?*
- *How will it benefit others?*
- *What will you do with the love you're going to manifest?*
- *What do you think your biggest block to manifesting more love is?*
- *Are there any other blocks, beliefs or old stories you need to change in order to manifest this into being?*
- *How can you bust through these blocks and open up to love?*

THE ENERGY RITUAL

To be able to attract, receive and hold the love you want, your heart chakra needs to be open and activated. This is often hard to do if you've been keeping your heart closed for a long time, so go at your own pace and open your heart in perfect timing for you. The following meditation can be done daily, weekly or whenever you feel the need to open up more fully to love.

Take yourself into a meditative state. Take a few deep breaths and come back to yourself and this moment. Visualise a pink flame of light in your heart centre. See this pink flame of light begin to grow with each deep breath until you feel your heart light expanding out to your shoulders, down into your belly and up towards your third eye.

Continue to see this pink flame of light growing until it fills your entire body and your auric fields. Stay here for a few moments, basking in the light of your own heart. See a protective blue flame of light appear in your heart space now. This blue light protects you from anything that isn't love.

See your heart opening up and expanding, opening to love. Feel the love from everyone who loves you pouring into your heart. Feel the love from the divine and the universe pouring into your heart. Feel the love from all the people who will love you in the future pouring into your heart. Now take some time to stay in this beautiful energy with your heart chakra lit up, aligned and activated.

When you're ready, come back to the present moment and place your hands on your heart, giving thanks for all that you have just experienced. Now move through your life knowing you have so much love to give and that you are deserving of receiving!

When you are ready, take three deep breaths into your heart, open your eyes and write about your experience in your journal.

MORE WAYS TO OPEN YOUR HEART CHAKRA:

- *Rub rose oil on your physical heart space twice daily.*
- *Wear a rose quartz necklace or a heart-shaped pendant at your heart.*
- *Chant YAM – the sound for the heart chakra.*
- *Be loving and kind to yourself and others.*

THE MAGIC RITUAL

As you perform this ritual continue to hold your intention in your mind and your heart.

You will need:

- *White light, sage smoke or an aura spray*
- *A small bowl or cup of water*
- *Roses or rose petals*
- *Oracle, tarot or prayer cards (optional)*
- *Paper and pencil*
- *Two white candles*
- *Two candle holders or heatproof plates*
- *Rose oil and herbs of your choice*

1. *Prepare your altar or sacred space, then prepare your energy. Clear yourself with white light, sage smoke or an aura spray. Take a few deep breaths and visualise yourself filled with pink light. Visualise a blue shield of light around you for protection and roots into the earth to ground you.*

2. *Place a small bowl or cup of water in the middle of your altar to honour the element of water. Place roses or rose petals around and/or into the bowl.*

3. *Place an oracle, tarot, prayer card or drawing representing what you'd like to manifest in front of the water.*

4. *Write your intention on a piece of paper and drop it into the bowl.*

5. *Dress the two candles in rose oil and herbs of your choice and place them either side of the bowl. One candle represents you, and one*

represents the love (another person, relationship or connection) you want to bring into your life.

6. *Call on divine assistance:* Thank you guides and angels, Goddess Aphrodite [and anyone else you'd like to call on] for helping me manifest the love I desire.

7. *Take some time here to ask for exactly what you'd like to manifest in your own words. Have a conversation with the divine, express what's in your heart and soul.*

8. *Light the candles. As the candles burn down, slowly begin to move them towards each other so that both candles (or candle holders) are touching as they burn to the bottom.*

9. *Keep the wax from the candles in a small bag or wrapped in a piece of cloth. Carry these wax remains with you and know that they will help you attract the love you're so ready for and worthy of.*

THE PRACTICAL MAGIC

If you're calling in new love and connection, make a plan to go to three places, events or gatherings where you think your people may be hanging out. Within the next 28 days (one moon cycle) try to meet at least three new people.

If you want to bring more love into your current relationships, plan three things you can do in this moon cycle to rekindle the spark. When someone invites you to a party, event or gathering, say yes. If you meet someone you like (romantically or otherwise), reach out to them and ask them if they want to connect.

Keep showing up, heart shining bright, and trust you'll attract all the most wonderful people and relationships to you!

MANIFESTING MONEY AND ABUNDANCE RITUAL

Whether you want to manifest a specific amount of money to pay for something you need or want, or if you just want an abundance of good things, this ritual can help you to unblock and open up the flow of prosperity in your life.

AFFIRMATIONS:

I am deserving and worthy of making, receiving and spending money.

I am a conscious, heart-centred custodian of money.

I am prosperous, abundant and do wonderful things for myself and others with my wealth.

I am a magnet for money.

THE CLEANSING RITUAL

Before you begin this money ritual it's a good idea to energetically clear yourself and any places where the flow of prosperity is being blocked. These blocks may be obvious or so subtle you may not even realise that you have them, but there are lots of simple and fun ways to start unblocking yourself and opening to the flow of prosperity, and you don't even need to consciously know what they are in order to clear them.

PURSE CLEANSE

See this purse cleanse as symbolic of your new start with the energy of prosperity.

- *Go through your purse or wallet and remove everything.*
- *Waft sage smoke through your purse or wallet and/or clean it with an aura spray.*
- *Throw away old receipts and anything that is taking up space or doesn't belong.*
- *Return your money and cards to your purse with respect and intention.*
- *Add in some small prosperity crystals and/or images of prosperity deities.*
- *Now keep your purse tidy and clear to keep the flow of prosperity moving in your life.*

YOUR MONEY STORY

Take a piece of paper and write out your money story. Write about your relationship with money as a child, as a teenager, as a young adult, and how it is now. Write about how you feel about money, how money has come into your life and the ways in which money has evaded you. Write about the ways you've spent money that have felt good and the ways that didn't feel good.

When you have finished writing your money story, take it outside, rip up the paper and set fire to it. As you watch your old story go up in flames, know that you are done with that story, that everything that has happened up to this point has been released and let go. You can now start a new story.

THE MINDSET RITUAL

Take some time to think about, meditate on and journal about your desires for more money.

GRAB YOUR JOURNAL!

In your journal answer these questions:

- *How much money do you want to manifest?*
- *Why do you want this money?*
- *How will this money change your situation?*
- *How will this money change your life?*
- *How will this money change you?*
- *What will you do when you have this money?*

Now it's time to get really honest about your relationship with money. Answer these in your journal or just meditate on them:

- *Where is your money going?*
- *Are you overspending, hoarding or managing your money well?*
- *How could you get into a better flow with how money comes into and out of your life?*

THE ENERGY RITUAL

The root chakra is located at the base of the spine and is the energy centre that aligns you with your thoughts, beliefs and feelings about the material world. Having an aligned root chakra not only helps you to attract abundance and prosperity, it can also help you feel more safe, secure and at home in your own body and life.

This is also the place where the Kundalini energy lies dormant. When you start to open up and activate the Kundalini, it moves from your root chakra up into all the chakras, aligning and connecting you to your highest available path in any moment.

On the spiritual journey we sometimes want to bypass these lower chakras to get to the third eye and crown so we can start to have a clearer connection with our guides and stronger spiritual sight, but if the root isn't balanced, grounded and anchored you can end up energetically tipping over.

A strong root chakra not only leads to a more positive connection with the material world and the ability to attract all that you need to be safe, secure and comfortable, it also lays a stable foundation for the higher chakras so they can activate and open up more easily and freely.

VISUALISATION

Take a few moments to get comfortable in your space. Take three deep breaths. Visualise yourself filled with and surrounded by white light and see a bright blue layer of light around you for protection.

Take your awareness to the root chakra at the base of the spine. See this chakra as a beautiful, ruby red, spinning ball of light. Now see a cord of light beginning to grow out from your root chakra and down into your legs and into your feet. Continue to send this cord of light down into the earth beneath you, see it passing through roots and rocks and all the layers of the Earth until you reach the heart of the Earth, the heart of Gaia, the heart of the great Earth Mother. Begin to wrap your roots around her heart, feel her heart beating and sending the highest love into your roots and up into your own heart. Feel a deep sense of safety, security and trust washing over you. Know that you are held, that you are safe, that all your material needs will always be met, that you are worthy of living the most prosperous and abundant life. Know that the great Earth Mother wants you to be safe and comfortable in this life. And remember that you are a part of the great Earth Mother, that as her heart beats, so does yours.

Feel yourself completely connected to the Earth, in total trust that you will always be provided for. Take a deep breath. Thank the great Earth Mother and begin to bring your awareness slowly back up through your roots, into your legs, into your root chakra and into your heart. Take a few moments to integrate this experience and write about it in your journal.

NATURE BATHING

Another powerful way to awaken, activate and align the root chakra is by spending time out in nature. Connecting with the natural world can help remind you that you are nature and you deserve to be provided for simply just by being here.

Go forest bathing, bush bathing or even park bathing. Walk through the trees, touch the trees, hug the trees! Take photos of flowers and just reconnect to the beauty of the Earth.

If you don't have much nature nearby, try to get your feet on some grass, sand or even dirt – whatever is available to you. Bring some pot plants into your home, grow some herbs on the windowsill and spend time with your animals, if you have them. Also be sure to eat lots of fresh fruit and veg and make plans to get into nature when you can.

As you spend time out in nature try to be as present as possible. Close your eyes and meditate, or just take a mindful walk. Don't multitask by listening to music or making phone calls, put your phone on silent and just be where you are.

THE MAGIC RITUAL: MONEY DRAWING SYRUP JAR SPELL

As you perform this ritual, continue to hold your intention in your mind and your heart.

You will need:

- *Washed jar with lid*
- *8 clean coins (or as many as you have)*
- *Maple syrup (the benefits of using maple syrup over honey are two-fold: one, it's vegan-friendly; two, it pours faster so makes money comes faster! If you can't get maple syrup any other kind of syrup or sugar works, or make sugar water)*
- *Dried herbs, such as oregano, saffron, marjoram, cinnamon*
- *Dried oranges*
- *Dried flowers – any will do, but yellow flowers or Chamomile work well*

- *A citrine, green aventurine or any other prosperity crystal (avoid pyrite as it won't do well in water or syrup!)*
- *A small piece of paper to write on*
- *A white, green, yellow or gold candle*

1. *Prepare your altar or sacred space and gather your supplies.*
2. *Prepare your energy. Clear yourself with white light, sage smoke or an aura spray. Take a few deep breaths and visualise yourself filled with gold light. Visualise a blue shield of light around you for protection and roots into the earth to ground you.*
3. *Call in your guides, angels and any other deities to help you with this spell (Goddess Fortuna or Goddess Lakshmi will work well for this). Simply say:* Thank you [name/s] for being with me as I work this spell. Thank you for overseeing this spell and aligning this magic towards my best and highest good.
4. *Take a moment to connect with your intention. Visualise yourself having the money you desire. Really* feel *yourself having this money and doing something wonderful with it.*
5. *Write your clear intention down on the piece of paper. You can write the monetary amount, or just:* money, prosperity, all my material needs are met – *anything that resonates with you.*
6. *Light some incense or sage and run it along the inside of your jar to clear it.*
7. *While holding the vision for the money you want to receive, consciously place each of the items into your jar starting with the coins, then layering the flowers, herbs and anything else you'd like to put in. Do this in the order that feels right. When the jar is full, top it up with syrup, sugar or sugar water.*
8. *Now drop (or squish!) the piece of paper with your intention into the jar.*

9. *Put the lid on the jar, and as you do this connect with the feeling of fullness, abundance and prosperity. Your jar is full, and soon your bank account will be too.*

10. *Light your candle and begin to drizzle wax along the edges of the lid of your jar, sealing it shut. It's a good idea to do this over a plate as wax may drip. Let some wax drop onto the top of the jar, then stick the base of the candle to the top. Make sure it's really stuck before releasing your hand.*

11. *Let the candle burn all the way down. If you need to take a break, snuff out the candle and relight it later.*

12. *Let your jar sit on your altar, shelf or somewhere safe for as long as it takes to receive the money. Once you have the money, or you intuitively feel that the spell no longer has any energy, break open the lid, bury the contents, wash the crystals and coins and keep them for another spell or spend them, and wash and reuse the jar for your next spell!*

THE PRACTICAL MAGIC

Check your bank accounts. Really look at how much money you have coming in and going out. Look at your expenses and make a budget. Stop paying for things you don't need, use or want. You may find that in doing this, extra money magically appears!

Honour and look after the money you do have. Donate to charity, no matter how small the amount. Doing this can open up the prosperity flow. Look for lost money – under the couch, foreign currency you haven't exchanged yet, in your tax return, and so on. When you start looking out for money in this way you may begin to find it on the street and in places you never thought to look before! Look into ways you could make some extra money. Sell something you no longer need on eBay, have a garage sale (bonus magic here as you'll be decluttering too!), tutor your neighbour's kids or start that side hustle. You never know where it may take you.

MANIFESTING WORK AND PURPOSE RITUAL

Work is such a big part of life and being able to manifest the dream job is a big goal for many. But it's not just a job most of us want; we want the feeling of living our purpose, doing something meaningful, spending our days doing what we love and what we really came here to do.

Although you may find your purpose in your job or career, there are many ways to fulfil your purpose. Perhaps your purpose is your family, your side hustle, your spiritual path, experiencing and enjoying life, caring for a loved one. There are so many reasons you are here, don't get bogged down in the idea that you're here to just do one thing. You're here to do, fulfil, create and manifest so many things.

In this section you can focus on manifesting a new job, your dream job, a better work situation or living more in alignment with your purpose – whether that's in your job or in another way. If you're already doing a job you love you could set your intention on a promotion or other better opportunities for your career.

AFFIRMATIONS:

I am already fulfilling my purpose and I'm manifesting new ways to move deeper into my dharma.

I live a meaningful life that makes a positive difference in the hearts of others.

I manifest my dream job, dream work opportunities and dream salary with ease.

I am a magnet for incredible work opportunities.

THE CLEANSING RITUAL

The greatest cleansing ritual you can do before manifesting a new work situation is to leave your old one, but that's not always possible, practical or advisable if you still need to pay the bills while you're working on calling in the new.

You can, however, energetically leave your old position or workplace behind. That doesn't mean you should go into work without caring about what you're doing, but you can energetically get one foot out the door.

THE VISUALISATION

Get yourself into a meditative state. Take a few deep breaths at your heart. See your heart lighting up with pink light and filling your body and aura. Visualise a bright blue shield of light around you.

Now visualise yourself leaving your current job. See yourself packing everything up from your desk, locker or anywhere else you leave things at work. Really tune into how it feels to do this.

Feel the gratitude for all this job has done for you and the excitement of what's coming next. See yourself saying goodbye to your co-workers, hugging and celebrating with the people you've connected with here. See any negative energy cords that attach you to your workplace, your role and people you work with being cleared, cut and dissolved with love.

Now see yourself walking out the door, saying goodbye and stepping into the new chapter.

Take as long as you like with this visualisation and keep coming back to it often, as you're manifesting this better work situation for yourself. If you struggle to visualise, write it down in words or draw pictures of you leaving, and so on.

As you do this, you're energetically releasing this job, any energetic ties you've created to the job or negative cords of attachment you have to the people who work there, and you should start to feel less trapped or stuck in your current role. You will start to remember it's only temporary and you will be ready to go as soon as a new job, role or situation appears.

It's so easy to get stuck in a job. Even when we dislike our jobs, they become comfortable, and we get comfortable in the discomfort, but this can create strong energetic cords, and until you clear them you may feel like you can't leave, even if the perfect situation comes along.

If you are currently unemployed you may not have so many ties to a job or workplace, but you can still do this practice, clearing yourself of any ties to past jobs, roles or workplaces and visualise yourself free and stepping into the new.

SHREDDING THE OLD

Another great cleansing practice is to burn, shred or recycle all your old work stuff. If you have old documents (make sure you don't need to keep them for tax purposes!), letters, notes, business cards, name tags, newsletters, uniforms, anything you no longer need from your current or past jobs, get rid of them. If you can't get rid of everything, just get rid of what you can.

If you're still hanging onto old schoolwork or university essays, let go of them too. And don't forget to clean up your digital files. Delete anything that you no longer need to make energetic space on your laptop.

THE MINDSET RITUAL

Take some time to think about, meditate on and journal about on your desires for a new work situation.

GRAB YOUR JOURNAL!

In your journal answer these questions:

- *How is your current work situation serving you?*
- *How is it not serving you?*
- *What blessings have you received from this job?*
- *What lessons have you learned?*
- *How can you use what you've learned to move forward now?*
- *What's your dream job?*
- *How would you most like to spend your work hours?*
- *What do you think your purpose is?*
- *What would you like your purpose to be?*
- *How could your work make a positive difference in the lives of others?*

THE ENERGY RITUAL

So many of us desperately want to figure out our purpose but struggle to know what it is. The truth is that you are already living your purpose. So much of what you are doing right now is your purpose. Your relationships, your own personal and spiritual development, even your current work situation is part of your purpose.

What many people want, however, is to feel a *deeper* sense of purpose. To feel like they *know* what their purpose is and to be working towards it, to do something *more*. But you already *know* what your purpose is and this next energy ritual involves waking up and becoming more conscious of what you already know deep within you.

Go back and look at your answers to the journalling questions above. Look at how you answered what you think your purpose is and what you want your purpose to be. Your dreams really are your purpose. That's why you feel them so deeply in your own heart. They are the reason you are here, they are what you came here to do. Your dreams may shift and change, but usually there is an aspect of them that stays the same. For example, you may have a dream to be a doctor, then it shifts into nursing or veterinary care, and then you may find yourself wanting to work as an energy healer. In this example, it's all part of a healing purpose. These are all just different ways to fulfil the same purpose.

VISUALISATION

Take a moment to get comfortable in your space. Take some deep breaths, centre and align your energy. Visualise a white golden light spinning above the top of your head, around the height of where your arms would be if you raised them above you. This is the soul star chakra. This chakra connects you to your higher self, the part of you that knows your soul contracts, your purpose, your best and highest path.

Take a few moments here connecting to this light. Whether you see it, feel it, or just know it's there, begin to see this light now opening up and pouring down into the top of your head, filling your mind with the knowing, the ideas, the direction, the guidance you need to help you remember your purpose and take your next steps. Trust you are receiving this whether or not you're consciously or subconsciously receiving it.

Bring this light down now into your heart. See the heart of your soul merging with the light of your heart. Feel your purpose dropping into and activating the heart. Take some deep breaths here, letting your heart fill with knowing. Now take this light further down and drop it into your belly. Let the light swirl around in your belly, really anchoring in your purpose.

See this light move down now into your feet. Feel your feet lit up and activated with this golden white light of your soul. Know that this is activating your feet with purpose, and that from now on you will always walk in the direction of your dreams and your purpose. Take a few moments here to really see yourself walking forward, finding your best and highest path and living your purpose, your dreams and your destiny.

When you are ready, take three deep breaths into your heart, open your eyes and write about your experience in your journal.

THE MAGIC RITUAL: SIGIL MAGIC

Working with sigils is a fun, creative and powerful way to amplify the energy of your intention.

You will need:

- *A piece of paper and a pen*

1. *Prepare your energy for the ritual. Take a few deep breaths. Reconnect with your soul star chakra. See that bright, golden-white light opening up above you and pouring down through your body and filling your aura. Visualise a blue light of protection around you.*
2. *Take a moment here to call in your guides, angels and any other beings you'd like to have support you with your magic. You may like to say something like:* Thank you [names] for being with me as I work my magic today. Thank you for helping me to find and fulfil my purpose and to help me find job opportunities that are in alignment with my soul's highest purpose and my highest destiny.
3. *Take your paper and write down a sentence that expresses exactly what you want. Take your time with this, re-write it as many times as you need to until you have a sentence that feels right. If you like you can simply write:* a job situation that is in alignment with my best and highest good.
4. *Now cross out all the vowels. Cross out any letter that appears more than once.*
5. *Write down the letters you have left. You can do this in either lower case or upper case. In the example above you would have:* j l w y or J L W Y.

6. *Now comes the fun part. Begin to use these letters to create your sigil. You can overlap them, spread them out into a circle, whatever you like. Start by making sure you have each letter included somehow, even if it's just a dot from a j or a loop from a y. As you get into the intuitive flow with this you may find your sigil starts to merge into something that doesn't resemble any of the letters you originally had. This is totally fine; just go where you're guided. One thing to consider, though, is that it can be useful if your sigil is simple enough to remember easily.*

7. *Draw out your sigil a few times until you feel like you have it as you want it.*

8. *Draw your sigil on a new piece of paper and visualise that it is glowing with light to activate it. You may even like to say:* This sigil is now activated and will always carry my intention, and so it is.

9. *Draw your sigil anywhere and everywhere to amplify your intention. You can draw it on paper and put it on your altar or anywhere else you will see it often. Take a photo of it and make it your lock screen. Draw your sigil on your wrist or somewhere hidden on your body. Draw it with a finger over job applications (online or paper copies), draw it over your desk or computer at work. Draw it over job ads, your social media posts, anywhere and everywhere that relates to manifesting your dream job situation.*

THE PRACTICAL MAGIC

If you want a new job, the best way to make that happen is to search for and apply for jobs. You may end up manifesting a job through a friend or a random meeting but searching and applying for jobs lets the universe know that you're serious about making it happen, and you may just find your dream job that way.

If you want a promotion or a pay rise, sometimes you just have to ask for it, or at the very least, let others in the workplace know what your goals are. You never know when you'll come up in conversation and someone may remember you saying you were interested in another opportunity.

If you want to move into working for yourself, start doing that now, not when you finally have time. Do a few hours on the weekend or a couple of evenings a week. Don't do so much that you burn out, but waiting until you have time often means never getting around to it and never making it happen.

If you want more success or recognition for your work, be vocal about and proud of what you're already achieving. Be confident, walk tall and speak your truth. If you don't speak your truth, how can you be heard?

MANIFESTING HOME AND HARMONY RITUAL

Our homes are our temples. Our living spaces are an extension of ourselves and often mirror back to us whatever is going on in our lives. When our homes are harmonious places that we love being in, we feel more relaxed, comfortable and at home in all areas of our lives.

Whether you are wanting to manifest more harmony in your current home or a new place to live, this section will help you to manifest it into being!

AFFIRMATIONS:

My home and home life is harmonious, peaceful and easy.

My home is my sacred sanctuary and I always feel at ease, at
peace and in joy in my space.

My current home serves me in wonderful ways while I call to me
a more aligned living situation.

I am a magnet for my best and highest living situation.

THE CLEANSING RITUAL

We've already touched on decluttering to clear the physical and energetic space so you can call more of what you want into your life, but when it comes to manifesting a better living environment, decluttering and physically cleaning and clearing your spaces really will shift the energy of both your home and you in magical ways.

Think of everything in your home as taking up space in your aura. Think of all those boxes like the old beliefs and stories taking up space in your mind. Clothes that no longer fit or make you feel good are like old habits that are holding you back.

If a moving truck of new boxes arrived at your home right now, where would they go? If you don't have space for the new, you may end up turning those boxes around without realising they contained everything you've been trying to manifest.

You don't have to clean and declutter everything all at once, just starting the process sends a powerful message to the universe that you are making space for your dreams. Do one room each day. Do a drawer each weekend if that's all you can manage. Keep a donation box somewhere in your home so you can immediately put things in it that you no longer need or want. Keep hold of sentimental items but consider how you could use or display them rather than have them sit in boxes just taking up space.

Notice how much better you feel when your home is less cluttered. Now you have more space and space for energy to flow and for all good things to find their way to you.

Whether you are planning to move out or just want your home to feel lighter, this will have a huge impact.

THE MINDSET RITUAL

Take some time to think about, meditate on and journal about your desires for a better home situation.

GRAB YOUR JOURNAL!

- *What do you love about your current home situation?*
- *What is challenging?*
- *Write down some potential solutions to these challenges.*
- *How do you want to feel when you're at home?*
- *What could you do to feel like that right now?*
- *What does your dream home or living situation look like?*
- *What's preventing you from living that dream?*
- *What's one step you could take right now to get closer to your dream home situation?*

THE ENERGY RITUAL:
A SPACE-CLEARING RITUAL

You can do this ritual any time you feel the energy of your home getting a little stuffy, stuck or heavy energetically.

You will need:

- *Sage or incense, or an aura spray*
- *Salt*
- *Essential oils*

1. *If you can, open all your windows and doors.*
2. *Play some high-vibrational music or mantras.*
3. *Light some sage or incense and begin to walk in an anti-clockwise direction while you gently waft the smoke through your space.*
   If you don't have or can't burn incense you can use an aura spray or make a simple spray using water, a few pinches of salt and a few drops of essential oils and gently spray around the space. Do this with intention. Focus on the space being cleared. You could say: May this space be clear, may all negativity be transmuted and released, may all stuck and stagnant energy be free *as you do this.*
4. *When you have finished, sit or stand in the middle of your space. Close your eyes and visualise the space filled with violet transmuting light and affirm:* This space is clear, this space is clear, this space is clear, and so it is.
5. *If you like you can also call in any angels, guides or deities to watch over your space and keep it protected, harmonious and high-vibrational. Archangel Zadkiel or Saint Germain will also be*

wonderful allies for transmuting and clearing energy in your home, within you or any time you feel the energy needs shifting.

THE MAGIC RITUAL: KITCHEN MAGIC

You can perform kitchen magic with any recipe you like as long as you're intentional. The best recipes for kitchen magic use organic and vegan ingredients as they are vibrationally higher, but as always you can use what you have or what you're intuitively drawn to.

The following is a simple sugar cookie recipe to give you an example of how to do this ritual, but don't forget you can do this with any other cookies, cakes, bread or even just when you're cooking dinner or making sandwiches!

You will need:

- *227g vegan butter*
- *150g sugar*
- *250g flour*
- *1 teaspoon vanilla essence*
- *Sprinkles or extra sugar*
- *Baking sheet*

1. *Tidy your kitchen – this ritual works best when you have a clear space to begin with. Press play on your high-vibrational playlist or mantras, preheat the oven to 165°C/325°F/gas mark 3 and prepare your ingredients.*
2. *Close your eyes and centre your energy. Take a few deep breaths in your heart space and connect with your intention.*

3. *Open your eyes and begin to mix the vegan butter and sugar together in a large mixing bowl with a mixer, stirring in a clockwise motion, bringing the intention towards you, or just use your hands and really squish your intention in. Connect with the idea that these cookies are a symbol of your manifestation. As you take these ingredients and turn them into delicious cookies, on an energetic level you are baking your dreams into being!*

4. *If you are manifesting harmony in your current home, connect with that intention. As you stir the ingredients see your home becoming more harmonious, full of love and peace. If you are wanting to manifest a new home, as you bake (or cook) visualise yourself stirring your new home towards you, or even visualise yourself baking these cookies in your dream home. Close your eyes for a moment and really see and feel yourself there.*

5. *Add in the flour and as you drop in the vanilla see your heart opening up and pouring your love into your cookie dough. Continue to stir clockwise and draw your intention towards you.*

6. *Begin to make 2cm balls of dough and place them on your baking sheet. Gently flatten them with your hand or a glass. Do this with the intention that you are shaping your dreams into reality.*

7. *Bake for about 15 minutes. During this time, as the scent of cookies starts to waft through your kitchen and your home, close your eyes and meditate on your intention for peace, harmony and happiness in your home or your new home.*

8. *Sprinkle on your sprinkles or a little extra sugar and let the cookies rest and cool.*

9. *Share the cookies with anyone you live with or anyone else you want to share these good vibes with. Let the energies of peace, harmony and love fill you all.*

10. *If you like, use the cookies for other magical rituals. Crumble a few cookies and sprinkle them outside by your front door or around the perimeter of your home with the intention that anyone who enters will bring harmony, peace and loving energy to the space. (This is not advisable if you have local rats or mice, though!)*

THE PRACTICAL MAGIC

When it comes to creating a harmonious home, we need to be mindful of what kind of energy we are personally bringing into our space. Your space is an extension of you, so take responsibility for what you put into it and remember you have the power to create the kind of space you want to live in.

If you've had a bad day, before you walk through your door take a deep breath and set the intention to leave as much of it outside as you can. If you have difficult relationships with the people you live with, take responsibility for your part. If you're more loving, kind and compassionate towards those you live with it can create a huge shift in your environment. People often respond with the same energy that is being sent to them, so send love and you may feel more coming back in return.

Keep your home clean and clutter-free. Put things away after you've used them. Don't collect new things you don't need, love or have no space for. Decorate your home in ways that make you feel good even if it's not on trend.

If you're manifesting a new home, make a plan. Figure out your budget, when you want to (or can) move, and start looking for places. Tell everyone you know that you're looking for a new place – someone might know somewhere that would be perfect for you.

If you need help getting out of your current situation and into somewhere better, reach out for support – from the universe, friends, family and any other services that could support you.

Practise gratitude for where you are right now. You may not be in your dream house just yet but being grateful for what you do have only brings more good things and opportunities your way.

THE BIGGEST SECRET: TRUST, SURRENDER AND NON-ATTACHMENT

The biggest secret to manifesting is not which herbs you use in your rituals, writing your intention down perfectly or calling in the right divine helpers. The real magic happens when you're able to find a balance between showing up for your dreams and letting go, trusting and surrendering.

When you can loosen your grip on what you want and trust that if it's in alignment with your best and highest good, it will happen, or if it's not, you'll be guided somewhere else, you will really be able to get into the flow of making your dreams come true. You'll be able to stop forcing things that aren't right for you and be open to wonderful opportunities coming to you that you haven't even thought of yet! And manifesting your dreams will finally feel easy.

When you are doing your practices and focusing on manifesting what you want, try to move into a place of non-attachment. Know that you will be absolutely fine whether this manifests for you or not. Ask that all your magic, spells and practices be done in alignment with your best and highest good and remember to end any practice with: *this or something better!*

It can be difficult to let go of attachment, especially when you're manifesting something you so desperately want. Non-attachment isn't about not wanting anything, it's just trusting that everything will be okay – that *you* will be okay whether you manifest this thing now, later or never, because if it's not right for you, you wouldn't want it anyway, and something else will always come in to take its place.

Don't get so focused on a specific idea, place, person, job or amount of money that you miss out so many of the other blessings available to you. If it's meant for you, it will find you. If it's not, be open to what is.

We are all just beings of light having a human experience. It's easy to get caught up in how we want this human experience to unfold, but what matters isn't really what you manifest, how much money you make, what job you do, or whether you're single or married, or living in a tiny house, trailer or mansion, it's how you live in each moment, how much love and joy you feel in the here and now and how you make the world a better place just by being here.

When you connect to that, manifesting really starts to become fun, because when it happens it's wonderful, and when it doesn't, you just find some other magic in the moment, or reconnect to the magic inside of you.

When you realise that the magic is always here because it's within you, both now and available in every future moment, that's when you really start living your dream life.

SOME TIPS FOR PRACTISING NON-ATTACHMENT

- *At the end of your manifesting rituals and practices, take a moment to remember that whether this manifests for you or not, you will be absolutely fine.*

- *Once you've done your manifesting practice, try to forget about it. Keep taking action where you can, but you don't need to keep asking for the same thing or doing a hundred different rituals with the same intention. You've put your order in, now you just wait, do your part, then go focus on something else. Think of it like applying for the job and then closing your laptop.*
- *Keep practising gratitude and noticing everything that is good in the here and now.*
- *Declutter. Keep letting go of things that you don't need, or go a step further and gift on items you actually do love and see how it makes you feel. Letting go of something you feel is important can help you realise it may not be as important as you think.*
- *Focus on your personal and spiritual development. Connect to your heart and higher self and remember your own divinity.*
- *And keep working on raising your vibration. The real secret when it comes to raising your vibration is that if you do it enough, you raise your entire consciousness too.*

TROUBLESHOOTING

Manifesting not working? Here are some reasons you may not be getting the success with your manifesting that you'd like.

IT HAS MANIFESTED, BUT NOT IN THE WAY YOU EXPECTED

Take a moment to notice if perhaps you have received what you asked for, but in a different way than you expected. For example, maybe you asked for a pay rise but instead you got a cheaper deal on your bills, leaving you with more money at the end of the month – same outcome, different way there. Or perhaps you asked for love and didn't find your soulmate (yet) but feel so much more self-love and deeper connection with your friends or family. Manifesting can happen in mysterious ways, so before you assume it's not working, pay attention to what's coming into your life in ways you weren't expecting.

TIMING

Manifesting can take time. Sometimes you may manifest almost instantly or within a few days or weeks, but depending on what you're asking for, how big it is, how big your belief is, and how in alignment or ready you are, it can take months or even years to manifest. But just because it hasn't happened yet doesn't mean it's not going to! Keep showing up and doing your part, and let it happen in perfect divine timing.

IT MIGHT NOT BE IN ALIGNMENT WITH YOUR BEST AND HIGHEST GOOD

Sometimes what our personality (or ego) self wants isn't the same as what our higher self, soul self or the divine part of us wants for us. Keep working on connecting with your soul star chakra, your higher self and your guides and angels and let them help guide you to what is your best and highest path even if you're not sure exactly what that is yet.

IS IT REALLY YOUR HEART'S DESIRE?

Check in with *why* you want what you're manifesting. You may be caught up in someone else's influence or projections. Check back in with your own heart and make sure you are manifesting what *you* want.

PROTECTION

Sometimes your guides will step in and stop you from manifesting something if it's going to send you off in a direction that is not in alignment with your best and highest good. Rejection can be protection and re-direction!

THERE'S SOMETHING BETTER COMING

If you're not getting what you've asked for, it may be because there's something better and even more wonderful than you can imagine right now on its way to you.

Always ask for this *or something better*!

ARE YOU BLOCKING YOURSELF?

A really common reason things don't manifest is because we are still carrying around old stories and limiting beliefs around not being worthy and deserving of the life of your dreams. Go back to the Preparing to Manifest section and keep working on believing in your own worth. And if it helps, here's a reminder – you really do deserve to live the life of your dreams. Say it to yourself every day until you start to believe it!

IS THERE SPACE FOR IT?

If what you've asked for has no space in your life, it's not going to be able to manifest, or if it does manifest you may not even notice it's there since there's so much other stuff taking up room. Energetically make space by using the clearing practices in this book so that when it arrives it can fit into your life.

ACCEPT HELP

Sometimes we need someone else in the physical world to help us manifest our dreams, so be open to letting people help you. Most of our big dreams don't happen on their own, they are collaborations and co-creations with others.

ARE YOU READY?

Sometimes our dreams are so big that we're just not yet ready to hold them. Keep working on yourself, on strengthening your aura, on your confidence and self-esteem. Keep focusing on your own personal and spiritual development. Keep showing up for yourself and your dreams and one day you *will* be ready to hold your biggest dreams.

GET OUT OF YOUR OWN WAY

While it's important to take action towards your dreams, sometimes you need to take a step back, trust and surrender and let the universe and your guides and angels do their thing.

HOLDING ON TOO TIGHTLY

Holding on too tightly to your dreams is like squashing a butterfly in your hands. You want to hold light and loose and let your dreams breathe.

Doing ritual after ritual and asking for the same thing a hundred times a day won't make your manifesting happen faster. Ask for what you want, do your part, then just try to relax, trust and surrender. I know it's easier said than done, but nothing blocks manifestation quite like desperation.

KEEP HOLDING THE VISION

You don't need to suffocate your dreams, but it's important that you don't stop believing. Keep believing that your dreams can come true, keep holding the vision in your mind's eye, on your vision board or altar and, most importantly, in your heart.

THE UNIVERSE HAS OTHER PLANS FOR YOU

Not everyone wants to live their highest destiny in this lifetime, but if you're reading this you are probably one of the few who do. When you commit to living your best and highest life, sometimes that means letting go of what you think you want and trusting in something bigger than yourself – whether that's the universe, the divine, or the divine light within you. Be open to going where you're guided.

WHEN ALL YOUR DREAMS COME TRUE

So, you've manifested your dreams – or at least some of them – now what? Well, now you keep dreaming.

Manifesting your dreams isn't something you just do once, then you live happily ever after, the end. Manifesting is something we'll all continue to do as long as we're on this planet. As one thing manifests, you'll already be working on the next thing and have plenty of ideas about what you want to manifest further down the road.

Remember to celebrate each dream when it manifests. Don't spend your life living in the future, waiting for the next thing to make you happy. Celebrating all that you've created, acknowledging and honouring your accomplishments and truly being thankful for all that you have received will unlock your ability to not only keep riding that wave towards manifesting what you want next, but it will also help you connect with all the blessings, happiness and peace in the present moment.

There will always be something new to want, a next thing to manifest, but you can look to the future with excitement and determination and still live and love in the here and now.

GRAB YOUR JOURNAL!

- *What has already manifested?*
- *How will you celebrate this?*
- *How will you look after yourself while you wait for your next dream to come true?*
- *How will you trust and surrender?*
- *How will you honour and celebrate yourself when you manifest your next dream?*

This is just the beginning. You have so much magic to make in your life, so much joy, love and opportunity coming your way.

I believe in you and your ability to live the life of your dreams. Believe in yourself and show up for your dreams, but more importantly, show up for yourself. Show up for the life you want to live, and you will find it.

May you manifest your dreams, may you have a lot of fun in the process and may you live a truly blessed, awakened and wonderful life.

And so it is.

With so much love,

Vix

x

ABOUT THE AUTHOR

Victoria 'Vix' Maxwell is the creator of New Age Hipster, a spiritual home for good witches, lightworkers, starseeds and spiritual seekers. A Priestess for present times, modern mystic and spiritual teacher in Converse sneakers, Vix supports her worldwide community in reconnecting to their own light, inner guidance and power through personal soul readings, spiritual development classes, tarot and oracle card-reading courses, Kundalini yoga workshops, spiritual business mentoring, podcast, award-winning blog and social media channels. Vix is the bestselling young adult fiction author of the *Santolsa Saga* series, author of *Witch, Please: Empowerment and Enlightenment for the Modern Mystic* and the *Angels Among Us* and *Goddesses Among Us* oracle decks.

To connect with Vix visit: www.newagehipster.co or @newagehipster333 on Instagram, Facebook and TikTok.

Please use the hashtag #ManifestYourDreamsBook to share your experiences with this book.

INDEX

abundance, *see* money/
    abundance/prosperity
action, 10, 11–12, 16, 17,
    29, 157–8
affirmations
  home/harmony, 184
  love/relationships, 160
  money/prosperity, 167
  positive influence/
    inspiration, 58–9
  work/purpose, 175–6
agate, 130
altars, 126–8, 140–1, 155,
    173
amazonite, 130
amber, 130
amethyst, 131
ametrine, 130
ancestors, 112, 150
  block to manifestation,
    81–3
angelite, 131
angels, 27, 89, 106, 111–12,
    153, 193
Aphrodite (goddess), 113,
    166
archangels, 51, 112

Ariel (archangel), 112
asking, 109–10
aura, 12, 50, 73, 82, 94, 145,
    164, 184, 195
  colours, 98
  elevating/expanding,
    97–8
  manifesting with, 99–100
  practice, 98–9
aura spray, 50, 125–6, 149,
    165, 168, 173, 186
aventurine, 130
awareness practice, 49

belief(s)
  blocking manifestation,
    20, 67–9
  in desires/dreams, 115–16
  limiting, 67–9, 73, 78
  limitless, 69–80, 73
  self-, 114–15
Buddhism, 9

calcite, 130
candle magic
  altar activation, 127–8,
    141

releasing negative
    influence, 56–8
  spells for manifestation,
    149–50, 165–6, 174
  see also fire ceremonies
capitalism, 21–2
carnelian, 130
cauldrons, 135
causal chakra, *see under*
    chakras
celebrities, 21
celestite, 131
chakras
  aligning, 102
  alignment meditation,
    104–6
  causal, 103, 106, 153–4
  crown, 38, 50, 82, 103,
    106, 170
  earth star, 103, 104
  heart, 103, 105, 163–4
  root, 103, 104, 105, 161,
    170–2
  sacral, 103, 105
  solar plexus, 103, 105, 161
  soul star, 103, 106,
    179–80, 181, 193

third eye, 103, 105, 164, 170

throat, 103, 105

charity, donating to, 74, 116, 156, 175

chrysoprase, 130

compliments, 85, 156

cookie recipe, 187–9

cooking, 65, 187–9

consumerism, 21–2

craft supplies, 135

crown chakra, *see under* chakras

crystals, 39, 114, 128–9, 140

  all-purpose, 129

  ethical sourcing, 124–5

  harmony/home, 130–1

  love/relationships, 129

  programming for manifestation, 147–8

  prosperity/abundance, 130

  spiritual growth, 131

  work/success, 130

dancing, 38

decluttering, 88, 175, 184–5, 189

deities, 13, 57, 112–13, 173

desires/dreams

  believing in, 115–16

  discovering, 63–4, 75–6

  evolution of, 62–3, 179

  manifesting, 17, 22, 60–2

  root of, 60–1

  see also manifesting/manifestation

dharma, 26, 74, 75, 175

diamond, 131

divine assistance, 10, 12–13, 14, 17, 110–13

  see also prayer

divine nature, 26

dreams, *see* desires/dreams

Earth Mother, 171

  see also Gaia

earth star chakra, *see under* chakras

eclipses, 124

ego, 9, 26, 27–8, 84, 114, 193

elementals, 113–14

emotions

  checking/monitoring, 108

  as guidance system, 106–7

  manifesting and, 155

energy

  clearing/protecting, 50–1

  cords, 161–2

  ritual, home/space-clearing, 186–7

  ritual, love/relationships, 163–4

  ritual, money/abundance, 170

  ritual, work/purpose, 179

  see also Law of Attraction

essential oils

  all-purpose, 131–2

  aura spray, 125–6

  harmony/home, 132, 186

  love/relationships, 132

  prosperity/abundance, 132

  ritual bath, 145–6

  spiritual growth, 132

  work/success, 132

ethical sourcing, 30–1, 124–5

eucalyptus oil, 56, 57

exercise, physical, 36

faeries, *see* elementals

fate, living in, 100, 101

fears, 83–4

fire ceremonies, 88–9, 128, 135, 168

flight-or-fight mode, 23

fluorite, 130

forest bathing, 171

forgiveness, 55–6

Fortuna (goddess), 113, 173

furniture, moving, 88

Gabriel (archangel), 112

Gaia, 104, 171

Ganesha (god), 113

generosity, *see* charity; giving

giving, and receiving, 156

gnomes, *see* elementals

goal setting, 154–5

  see also desires/dreams

goddess box, 152

gods/goddesses, 112–13

gratitude, 41, 85–6, 176, 190, 197

  expressing, 44

  invocation, 102

  jar, 43

  journal, 43

  list, 45

  morning practice, 43

  night practice, 44

  photo album, 44

  prayer, 42

  scrap book, 45

grimoire, 128

guides, spirit, 13, 89, 106, 111, 114, 135, 173, 193

guilt, releasing, 73–4, 75–6

happiness, and wealth, 22

heart

  chakra, *see under* chakras

  manifestation from, 27–8

  vs ego, 27–8

  see also love/relationships

hematite, 130
herbs/spices
  all-purpose, 133
  harmony/home, 134
  love/relationships, 133
  prosperity/abundance,
    133
  spiritual growth, 134
  work/success, 134
  see also rosemary; sage
Highest Destiny, 100–1
Hinduism, 113
home/harmony
  affirmations, 183–4
  cleansing ritual, 184–5
  crystals for, 130–1
  energy/space-clearing
    ritual, 186–7
  herbs for, 134
  kitchen magic, 187–9
  mindset ritual, 185
  oils for, 132
  practical magic, 189–90
howlite, 130

incense, 50, 126, 127, 134,
    142, 147, 149, 186
influencers, 48, 49
inspiration, 56, 60
intuition, 4, 12, 64, 80, 129,
    133

jade, 130
jasper, 131
jealousy, 75–6
journalling, 5, 128
judgement, 21, 76–7,
    109
  discernment over, 78
  practice, 77–8

karma, 25, 26
Kundalini yoga
  energy, 170

Highest Destiny, 100–1
  meditation, 86–7
kyanite, 131

labradorite, 131
Lakshmi (goddess), 113,
    173
Law of Attraction, 24–5,
    94–5
  practices, 95–7
Law of Free Will, 25
Law of Grace, 45–6
lepidolite, 130
life purpose, 26, 178,
    179–80
  see also dharma; work/
    purpose
love/relationships
  affirmations, 160
  cleansing ritual, 160–1
  crystals for, 129
  energy ritual, 163–4
  herbs/spices for, 133
  magic ritual, 165–6
  mindset ritual, 162–3
  oils for, 132
  practical magic, 166
  visualisation, 161–2
  see also heart; self-love

magical people, connecting
  with, 156–7
magical spaces, see sacred/
  magical spaces
magical tools, see
  manifesting tools
mala beads, 58, 65
manifesting/manifestation
  author's journey, 1–4
  blocks, see manifesting
    blocks
  celebrating, 196–7
  conscious, 29–31
  deities/angels for, 112–13

dharma/karma and, 26
four elements to, 10
for others, 115–16
from the heart/ego and,
    27–8, 32, 47–8, 59, 62, 63
in a challenging world,
    31–2
meaning, 9–10
mental health and, 2, 15,
    27
monitoring during day, 30
myths, 15–18
practices, all-purpose,
    136–9
practice, taking action,
    157–8
preparing for, 59–63
rituals, see rituals
setbacks, 24
symbols/sigils for, 70,
    150–1, 181–2
times, best for, 119–22
times, to avoid, 123–4
tools, see manifesting
  tools
trauma and, 23
troubleshooting, 192–6
wish list, 144–5
with emotion, 155
  see also home/harmony;
    love/relationships;
    money/abundance/
    prosperity; work/
    purpose
manifesting blocks
  ancestral, 81–3
  comparison/competition,
    75–6
  evolution of 89–90
  fears, 83–4
  general practices for
    clearing, 87–90
  guilt, 73–4
  judgements, 76–8

past life, 78–9
privilege, 19–21
to receiving, 85–6
worthiness/self-esteem,
71–2
manifesting tools
altars, 126–8, 140–1, 155,
173
candles, *see* candle magic
crystals, *see* crystals
goddess box, 152
herbs/spices, *see* herbs/
spices
oils, *see* essential oils
sourcing, 124–5
tarot cards, 37, 65, 135,
140, 148
vision boards, 141–4
mantras, 58, 65, 89, 152–3
media, positive *vs* negative,
52–3
meditation
chakra alignment, 104
clearing ancestral blocks,
82–3
daily, 64, 65
heart chakra activation,
163–4
journey to the past, 72–3
to practise receiving,
86–7
mental health
consumerism and, 22
manifesting and, 2, 15,
27
Merlin, 113
mermaids, 113, 114
Michael (archangel), 51,
112
mindfulness, 36
mirror work, 36
money/abundance/
prosperity
affirmations, 167

cleansing ritual, 167–8
crystals for, 130
energy ritual, 170
herbs for, 133
mindset ritual, 169
money drawing spell,
172–4
money story, 168
nature bathing, 171–2
oils for, 132
practical magic, 174–5
visualisation, 170–1
moon, setting goals by, 155
moonstone, 131
Morgan le Fay, 112

nature
bathing, 171–2
cycles, and goal setting,
154–5
spirits, *see* elementals
negative influence
awareness of, 49
clearing/protection from,
50–8, 63–4
forgiveness and, 55–6
friends/family, 54–5
media, 52–3
social media, 48, 53–4
negative thinking, 17, 38
New Thought and
Theosophy, 9
non-attachment, 190–1
tips for practising, 191–2

obsidian, 131
ocean ritual, 89–90
oils, *see* essential oils
oracle cards, 135, 140

palo santo, 50, 126, 127,
134
periodot, 130
planets, 123

positive influence
friends/family, 54–5,
156–7
helping others, 74
media, 52
social media, 53
through affirmations,
58–9
positive thinking, 15
toxic, 23–4
power
calling back/owning,
92–4
to change, 91–2
of words, 108–9
prayer, 13, 125, 151–2
privilege, 19–21
prosperity, *see* money/
abundance/prosperity
purpose, *see* work/purpose
pyrite, 130

Quan Yin (goddess), 113
quartz, 128, 129, 130, 131,
147, 164

receiving
giving and, 156
meditation to practise,
86–7
reiki, 37, 72
relationships, *see* love/
relationships
retreats, spiritual, 64–5
retrogrades, 123
rituals
bathing, 145–6
enjoy yourself, 75
home/harmony, 183–90
love/relationships,
159–66
money/abundance,
167–75
ocean, 89–90

releasing past life vows, 80–1
work/purpose, 175–83
root chakra, *see under* chakras
rosemary, 56, 132, 134

sacral chakra, *see under* chakras
sacred/magical spaces, 38, 80
preparing, 125
see also altars
sage, 50, 56, 126, 127, 134, 147, 149, 165, 168, 173, 186
Saint Dymphna, 27
Saint Germain, 186
Sandalphon (archangel), 112
security, 23, 61, 171
selenite, 131
self, higher, 113
self-belief, 114–15
self-blame, 15, 24–5
self-care, 36–7
self-employment, 183
self-esteem, 23, 71–2, 195
self-judgement, 76–7
self-love, 15, 24, 35–6, 38, 55, 56, 95, 96, 159
shredding, 177–8
sigils, *see* symbols/sigils
sleep, 36, 44
smiling, 95–6
social media, 21, 48, 108, 109, 182
positive *vs* negative, 53–4
taking a break from, 36, 64, 66
sodalite, 130
solar plexus chakra, *see under* chakras

soul star chakra, *see under* chakras
spices, *see* herbs/spices
spirituality/spiritual growth
crystals for, 131
herbs for, 134
myth, 16
oils for, 132
retreats, 64–6
spirit guides, 13, 89, 106, 111, 114, 135, 173, 193
sprites, *see* elementals
suffering, 16
sunstone, 130
symbols/sigils, 70, 150–1
work/purpose ritual, 181–2

tarot cards/reading, 37, 65, 135, 140, 148
third eye, *see under* chakras
thoughts
negative, *see* negative thinking
positive, *see* positive thinking
throat chakra, *see under* chakras
tiger's eye, 130
topaz, 130
trauma, 23
turquoise, 131

Uriel (archangel), 112

vibrations
aligning for manifestation, 10, 12, 17, 122, 158
raising, 23, 24, 37–9, 41, 153
visualisation for high, 40–1

water ritual, 40
victim-blaming, 16
vision boards, 141–4
digital, 144–5
visualisation, 57, 104, 138–9
high-vibe, 40–1
love/relationships ritual, 161–2
money/abundance ritual, 170–1
work/purpose ritual, 176–7, 179–80
vows, past life, 79–81

wealth, and happiness, 22
Witch, Please: Empowerment and Enlightenment for the Modern Mystic (Maxwell), 3
witchcraft, 9
words
power of, 108
saying out loud, 136
writing down, 137, 139
work/purpose
affirmations, 175–6
cleansing ritual, 176, 177–8
crystals for, 130
energy ritual, 179
herbs for, 134
magic ritual (sigil), 181–2
mindset ritual, 178–9
oils for, 132
practical magic, 182–3
visualisations, 176–7, 179–80

yoga, *see* Kundalini yoga

Zadkiel (archangel), 186